Murders of Necessity

Acknowledgements

My thanks to Sheilah for all her help, ideas, and hours of proof reading and editing.
Without her hard work this book would never have been finished.

Thanks also to Emma for previewing the book and her invaluable feedback

CHAPTER 1

Morris Barnack woke with a start but didn't know why. Was it something he heard? Everything seemed quiet now. He looked at his wife sleeping next to him. Usually, she would wake at the sound of anything.

He decided it was nothing and turned over, pushing the bedclothes down because he felt hot. It had been a muggy day, which was rare on the North Norfolk coast. Usually, even on a hot summers day, there was a refreshing breeze coming off the North Sea.

He was just beginning to drop off when there was a noise from downstairs in the shop. He lifted himself from the bed onto one elbow. He was wide awake now. He touched Gladys' shoulder and whispered, 'There's someone in the shop.'

'Be careful,' said Gladys. She knew what a hot-head Morris could be.

'It's those damn kids again, and this time they have gone too far. Writing obscenities on the front door is one thing, but coming into the shop is something different. It's burglary,' he said.

Gladys wished that she had insisted that they should have a phone extension upstairs. Morris said it wasn't worth the extra money the Post Office was asking, and he didn't want business calls disturbing him when the shop was closed. If that was the case why did he run downstairs to answer calls, even in the middle of eating his dinner?

He got out of bed and picked up the baseball bat that he had propped against the wall. Morris was a small, studious-looking man, and certainly not the sort of flamboyant man who you often find owning Antique shops. He was more like a clerk, possibly in a bank or an accountants office. Being meticulously honest, some people might say pedantic, the sign over the shop door said, 'Antiques, Memorabilia and Collectables.' Morris did not want any customer to go away from his shop, feeling that they had been mis-sold.

He walked as quietly down the stairs as he could. His sizeable shop was in an old Victorian building, just off Church Street, in the small seaside town of Cromer in Norfolk. Several of the steps on the stairs groaned, even under his comparatively light weight, so he carefully placed his feet at the sides of the steps to reduce the noise as much as possible. The element of surprise is vital when you are dealing with a gang of hooligans, he thought.

There was a door at the bottom of the stairs that led into the shop. He opened it cautiously and stepped inside. He couldn't see anyone and moved further into the shop.

Suddenly, he heard a noise behind him and turned to see a huge man charging towards him. Instinctively, he swung the bat that was in his right hand and caught the attacker on the side of his head, knocking him sideways into a display stand of willow pattern crockery.

Morris was on the point of giving the big man another clout with the bat when he was grabbed from behind by someone who seemed equally large. He wrapped both his arms around Morris and was trying to drag him away. He was too strong for Morris who was lifted off the floor kicking and shouting.

The other brute was climbing to his feet and trying to stand on unsteady legs. He was cursing Morris and inspecting the blood that was coming from his left ear. He looked at the blood on his hand, screamed at Morris again and just charged at him, knife in hand.

The last thing Morris heard was the man who was holding him shouting 'No Arthur, no.' The knife punctured Morris' heart.

Arthur stood looking at Morris, lying on the floor, a flow of blood spreading out from around the body. His mouth was sagging open, and he seemed to be having difficulty in assimilating what had happened. His mouth sagged even wider, as he looked down at the blood-covered knife in his hand.

'You fucking idiot,' said Shay, shaking his head in disbelief. 'You absolute, total fucking idiot. What did Micky say? Give him a bit of a fright? Let him know that he's got to stop mouthing off about us and the business. Well, you've certainly done that. What the fuck did you do that for?' He pointed to where Morris lay, 'and why pull a knife on him?'

'I thought it would put the wind up him,' Arthur said.

'And you thought that you and me breaking in here, and jumping out on him when he came down the stairs, wouldn't be enough to scare the hell out of him? Look at the size of us and the size of him? We smack people around for a living, and he's a piddling little shopkeeper. What the hell is Micky going to say about this.' Shay turned his back on the scene and started to pace up and down the shop.

'Don't forget he had the bat. He attacked me first," Arthur said sullenly.

'Only because you were charging at him with a knife. What did you expect him to do, a neat sidestep like a fucking bullfighter?'

They heard tentative footsteps on the stairs. Both of them turned and ran to the door and out onto the street. It was after midnight, and there was nobody around. They had parked their car around the corner. They got into it, and Shay drove carefully through the empty streets.

He turned onto the Norwich Road, and they soon left Cromer behind.

'Where are we going?' Arthur asked.

'We'll find somewhere to park up where nobody can see the car, kip in it overnight, and then make a big deal about our arrival back at the house round about 12.30 tomorrow. Make it look like we have been away. As far as I could tell, nobody saw us go into or come out of the shop. His misses was halfway down the stairs so she couldn't have seen us. And nobody was around when we got into the car and drove out of town.'

Arthur sat silent for a few minutes and then said, 'You're an absolute bloody genius Shay. I could have never thought of that.'

Shay shook his head. 'No, I don't suppose you could, but that doesn't make me a genius mate. If I had any sense at all, I would have done the job by myself.'

CHAPTER 2
Six weeks later.

Martin Yates had a quick rise to success as a newspaper and now magazine editor. 'Inside London' was a magazine for the rapidly growing group of young, successful people throughout the country, but especially in the home counties. It was mid-1960s England. Suddenly the young men and women were setting trends in fashion, music, the arts, retail and even crime. The magazine was designed to appeal to the adventurous and highlight almost anything that was anti-establishment.

Most of the stories of excess, which were intended to shock, amuse and titillate, he did not like. But he wasn't paid to like what he was publishing; his pleasure came from just doing the job of editing a publication that was on the side of the revolution that was taking place. That was what he loved. It was only two years ago that he was editing a local newspaper in Peterborough, which did its job of keeping people informed, giving opportunities to express opinions and promoting a feeling of community. But that was based on well-established standards, where people knew their place in society.

Now, he saw himself as part of the entertainment industry, when who's on the way up and who's on the way down was an important issue. Even more important was whose party was the most outrageous and, of course, who is sleeping with who. The fact that Martin didn't care, and certainly never mixed with any of that particular group, did not matter at all. It was 1964, and this is what people wanted to read. He was a professional, and he was going to give them what they wanted and make a success of 'Inside London.'

However, it did give him particular pleasure when he could work with people he knew, trusted and liked. Today, he had a tip-off about a crime story, and the freelancers he used to cover crime were a young couple that had worked for him on the Peterborough newspaper. Emily and Steve had worked together on a particularly difficult case, involving several murders, which put them both in a highly dangerous situation. At the time, Emily was just 23 and a trainee journalist.

Through the work they did on that story, Emily and Steve became quite well known, and they soon quit the paper to work freelance. When Martin got the job editing the magazine, he invited Steve and Emily to join his freelance team. They were happy to accept and had worked for him on several occasions. He called them two days ago and asked them to come to a meeting at his office in Long Acre, not far from Leicester Square.

The offices were above a lady's fashion shop, that looked as though it had seen better days. It amused Emily, every time they came to Martin's office. The irony of the drab suits and dresses that had changed little since the end of the war, compared to the bright and daring clothes that featured on the pages of 'Inside London'. It was a different world now and Emily, like many young women of her age, was going to make the most of the freedom and excitement that was happening here, in London.

Emily and Steve climbed the dark and dingy stairs that led up one flight and pressed the bell on the dilapidated door, which had been painted blue, but also showed several different colours where the layers of paint had chipped.

The door was opened by Eileen, Martin's secretary. She was a short, stocky and very smiley woman, who was always very welcoming. Inside was like another world. The furniture was sleek and new, the walls painted in bright primary colours, and there were huge photographs of the top celebrities that had featured in the magazine. There was only a handful of staff inside. The owners of the magazine believed in keeping staff numbers to a minimum and using the best freelancers available.

Martin was sitting on the edge of a desk talking to one of the staff. As soon as he saw Emily and Steve, he stood up and came smiling towards them. He kissed Emily and shook Steve's hand. He looked at his watch and said, 'That is good timing. Or have you been waiting outside for half an hour?'

'The coffee bar just around the corner,' Emily said. 'Steve hates rushing anywhere and I quite like leaving plenty of time and arriving at the meeting nice and relaxed.'

'The trouble is,' Martin said, 'this town is not built for relaxing. It's one huge rush hour that starts at around seven in the morning and stops about two the following morning.'

They walked through to Martin's office, which was small, but adequate. He sat at his desk, and Emily and Steve sat facing him.

'So, what have you got for us?' asked Steve.

'Something of a challenge, I think, but who knows. It could be easy, but these jobs seldom are,' Martin said.

'We do like a challenge, but would prefer it to be easy.' Emily smiled.

'Okay, I'll tell you what I know. I have a friend in the police who said that they are really under pressure at the moment because of a spate of burglaries and muggings, targeting high-end jewellery and other valuables. Of course, this means that the gangs who are carrying out these thefts are targeting people who are wealthy and have a good deal of influence. So, the police are really under pressure to catch them and put them behind bars.'

'Surely, if the London police can't catch them, we don't stand much of a chance?' Steve said.

'Ah, that's where another friend of mine comes in. He is on the opposite side of the fence to my police friend. He didn't know a lot, but what he did know he was happy to share with me because these gangs are making life difficult for him and his mates. So, they would welcome someone putting a stop to it, but as you can imagine, they can hardly call the police up and tell them.'

'What did he tell you?' asked Emily, somewhat taken aback that Martin would know such people.

'He thinks that this is being run by a man, or a 'geezer' as he put it, who used to work in London and control several of these small gangs who specialise in breaking into 'nobs' houses, where the takings are really worthwhile.'

'Who is this Mr Big,' Steve said with a grin at Martin's efforts to sound like a London gangster.

'He either wouldn't or couldn't name him, but he said that the man has left London and now runs things from somewhere on the North Norfolk coast,' Martin said.

'Did he say where?' asked Steve.

'No, he didn't know that, but he said it was just a small town.'

'Well, there's not a lot to choose from,' said Steve. 'Just Hunstanton, Wells, Sheringham or Cromer. Let's hope its Cromer because that's my hometown.'

'Is it really?' said Martin, thinking that Steve was just pulling his leg.

'Yes, honestly,' said Steve. 'It's where I grew up, and my mother still has a B&B there.'

'Well there you go,' said Martin, 'you've got a head start.'

'At least I won't go blundering in not knowing anyone or anything. And Emily will be pleased; she loves being with my mum.'

'Do I detect a note of sarcasm?' Martin asked.

'No, said Emily, 'she's great. A strong woman, who is not afraid to say what she thinks, but is also extremely kind.'

Steve shrugged his shoulders. 'What can I do when they gang up on me.'

Martin laughed, 'I feel sorry for you Steve. But back to business. Are you both up for the job?'

'Just one question?' said Emily. 'Why are you getting us to go up there and not just passing on that information from your friend to the police.

'Because this is our story. We can get the whole thing written and published before anyone else gets a sniff of it. It's classic investigative journalism. This is a big deal for you and Steve. Everyone will know your names if you can pull it off.'

As they walked away from the meeting Emily said to Steve, 'I'm not sure I want everyone to know my name, are you?'

'No,' Steve laughed. 'I think the bright lights and big city are going to Martin's head. But you can see why he thinks this could be a great story. It's just that he doesn't seem to be taking into account the risks we are taking.'

'What do you think?' asked Emily. 'We can still say no, but we do like a challenge.'

'Yes, let's give it a go, and if it starts to get a bit hairy, we can get out quick.'

She squeezed his hand as they walked towards Leicester Square underground station. 'You do realise we are becoming danger junkies, don't you?' They both laughed a little nervously.

CHAPTER 3

When Emily and Steve arrived back at Peterborough station, they walked quickly back to their apartment, which was barely a quarter of a mile away. It was in a large Victorian house at the town end of Lincoln Road. They had the first-floor apartment, which was spacious, but safe to lock-up and leave when they were on one of their assignments.

They were anxious to call Steve's mother and find out if she knew anything about this man who had apparently moved to Norfolk to run his team of housebreakers and muggers from a distance.

'Hello, mum.'

'Hello Steve, is Emily okay?'

'Yes, she fine.' He nodded and smiled at Emily. His mother always seemed to be concerned about Emily when he called. He worried when he first took Emily to meet her, thinking that they were both very forceful characters, who liked to get their way by using persuasion and persistence. But they hit it off straight away and loved each other's company. There were times when he felt a little left out, but then he thought that it was better if the two people he loved most in the world got on together, rather than having to keep them apart.

'We might be coming to North Norfolk soon; working that is.'

'I'm fully booked for the next few weeks, could you leave it until later.'

'No, it's a story we have to look into quickly. But don't worry about accommodation, we will be on expenses and will book in anywhere we can get.'

'Yes, but Emily will want somewhere nice.'

'We will get somewhere nice,' Steve said, trying not to sound irritated.

'I'll have a word with the manager of the Hotel de Paris. I've helped him out on several occasions, and he is a lovely man. Italian, I think.'

Steve knew when he was beaten. 'That's very good of you mum, but there is also something else I want to ask you. I know this sounds strange but has anyone new come to live in the town recently. He might look as if he doesn't belong. A big city type, probably keeping a low profile at the moment?'

'No, not that I know of, but I am a bit out of touch with things. You know I've never liked gossip. And there is always plenty to do with the B&B. I tell you what I will do though; I'll go next door and ask Mrs Johnson. There is nothing that goes on in Cromer that she doesn't know about. She's a lovely person. She is just very interested in people. I'll call you back in half-an-hour.' And with that, the line went dead.

Steve looked at Emily, shook his head in disbelief and put the phone back in its cradle.

'We are going to have to be very careful when we go to see her or she will be taking over the story herself.'

Emily laughed. 'You've got to admit; she is nothing if not enthusiastic.'

True to her promise Steve's mother rang back after only twenty-five minutes.

'Yes, Steven,' she said excitedly. 'There is someone new. Mrs Johnson thinks his name is Micky somebody and there is also a very attractive wife. They have bought a big house on Cliff Drive, and you know what some of those houses are like. Apparently, it has a pool as well.'

"Okay, that sounds very promising. I am going to put Emily on the phone now because she has something very important to tell you.'

'Oh, how lovely, thank you Steven.'

Emily was looking puzzled as Steve held the phone out towards Emily, his hand covering the mouthpiece. 'Tell her not to speak to anyone about this,' he said.

'You tell her,' said Emily.

Steve stood up and placed the phone into Emily's hand. 'When has she ever listened to anything I say.'

'Hello mother, how are you,' said Emily cheerfully. Mother was the agreed way of distinguishing between her mum and Steve's mother.

'I'm well thank you, and it's lovely to hear from you, Emily.'

'Yes, I am looking forward to seeing you again. It's a pity we are working, but I am sure we will find time to drop in. But I have something very important to say to you,' Emily said in her most earnest voice.

'What's that my dear.'

'The people we are going to be looking for are not nice. Steve and I are going to have to be very cautious and keep a low profile. What Steve has discussed with you has to be a secret between us.'

'And Mrs Johnson of course,' Steve said with a sigh.

'Oh,' said Steve's Mother. 'I understand completely. Just between us.'

'Okay then, we'll see you tomorrow.' Emily put the phone down.

'I think she understands the situation,' Emily said to Steve.

'Yes, she'll be alright now you have spoken to her. If I'd said that to her we'd still be arguing.'

CHAPTER 4

Emily and Steve drove to Cromer in their bright Red Triumph Spitfire. It was an indulgence, bought following a particularly big story they had investigated for a national newspaper. Before then their only means of transport was a Lambretta scooter, which was Steve's pride and joy, but completely impractical for work.

It was a pleasant early September day, with a light breeze and slightly misty sun to give just enough warmth to fold back the canopy and enjoy the fresh air.

They made a stop at a roadside café just passed Wisbech and arrived in Cromer around midday. Emily felt the same surge of excitement that she used to get as a little girl when they came down the Holt Road and saw the sea sparkling on the horizon. Steve drove through the town and stopped outside his mother's B&B.

She greeted them in the front garden, which had now been given over to a gravelled car park. They walked around to the side of the house and went in through the door to the small area that Iris Moon, Steve's mother, had allowed herself for her accommodation.

'Is it my imagination or does your flat get smaller every time I come to visit?' Steve asked.

'Well, I am always fully booked, so I decided to make another guest room in the loft. You get a lovely view of the town from there. But that meant I had to enlarge the breakfast room, so we had to take a little off my lounge. But it's no problem,' she replied.

Steve knew only too well that behind the diffident person that his mother portrayed, there was a very sound and determined businesswoman. His father had worked in a bank in Cromer before the war, but was called up in the early days and was killed in Libya a couple of years later. The war years were difficult for them both, but thanks to her strength they survived having numerous evacuees in the house and a few years after the war, faced with the fact that she either had to sell the house or make some money out of it, she chose the latter.

She started by letting out two rooms and then gradually converting it to six bedrooms, in addition to her own accommodation. 'So, that's seven rooms now, how do you manage?' he asked.

'There were two very nice girls down the road who were looking for jobs, and you know how difficult that can be around here. They clean the rooms, change the bedding and take it in turns to help me with the breakfast. We manage pretty well between us,' she said.

'You will be taking over the Hotel de Paris soon,' laughed Steve.

'No thanks, I am very happy with what I have. But that reminds me, I spoke to the manager of the Hotel de Paris, as I said I would, and he has a room reserved for you.'

'That's great,' said Steve. 'You must have influence to get a room at such short notice.'

'He is a very nice man, and we have become good friends,' she said. Steve noticed that his mother was blushing slightly, but before he could say anything, she said, 'And Emily, you're looking as lovely as ever. How are you?' she asked.

'I'm very well thank you. I was just admiring your garden. Surely you don't have to look after all that yourself.'

'No I don't, I forgot to mention George. He looks after that for me.'

'How did you find him?' asked Steve.

'He's lives here now. You remember the small barn that was in the back garden. Well, I had it done up and turned it into a bedsit for George. He and his wife used to come for their holiday every year in June. From Norwich. Well, his wife died, quite suddenly I think, and George was rather lost without her. He decided to retire from his work on the railways and was looking for somewhere to stay in Cromer.

'He just wanted a little place, and he was going to do gardening work to top up his pension. I offered to have the barn converted and kept the rent low, and in return, he does the garden. He picks up other work as well. He's lovely man. You'll have to meet him.'

Steve walked over to the window. 'Yes, I don't think I've seen the garden looking better. The lawn is immaculate.'

'So, that is quite enough about me, how are you getting along now that you are freelance.'

Emily decided that she would answer, to save Steve from everything he says being challenged. 'Very well. The jobs are irregular, which can sometimes be worrying, but the fees are so much higher than a regular job, that it makes up for any uncertainty.'

Iris nodded her understanding and then asked, 'Isn't it going to be difficult, carrying out your investigation when Steven is so well known around here.'

'Yes, it's not going to be easy, but we are just here to have a holiday. That's what we will be telling everybody. The people we know we can trust like you and Eric will know why we are here, but to the others, we are having a holiday.'

His mother smiled. 'Yes, I see Eric quite regularly. He does any plumbing jobs that I have, and he's still the same old laid-back Eric. Nothing seems to rattle him at all.'

Iris turned to Emily. 'He was Steven's best friend at school and very bright, but he decided he wanted to learn a trade and stay in the town. It's a place like that. Some people never want to leave.'

'Yes,' said Emily, 'Steve has told me about Eric. I'm looking forward to meeting him.'

'While we are trying to get the information we need for this story, we will not be able to come here, Steve said. The people we are dealing with are outsiders and will not know our relationship. We want to keep it that way as long as possible. And they are also ruthless, and we don't want to put anyone in danger.'

'What about Emily and you Steven. You will be in danger.'

'We will, but this is what we do for a living. We have learnt a lot about staying safe and keeping a low profile since that first job we did together in the fens. That was a bit too close for comfort, but there will always be dangers, so we have to be aware at all times. It helps working together, we can look out for each other, and you build up a sixth sense about situations.'

'Well, you both be very careful,' Iris said.

'We will,' said Emily.

They walked towards the car and Iris was about to close the door,' when she said, 'I know what I was going to tell you. I just wondered if your investigation has anything to do with the Antique dealer who was murdered in his shop.'

It stopped Emily and Steve instantly.

'Here in Cromer?' Steve asked.

'Yes,' Iris replied, 'His shop is just off Church Street.' She saw the look of surprise on their faces. 'It was in the local papers for a few weeks, but I haven't seen anything recently. They seemed to think it was a burglary that went wrong. But I haven't heard of any arrests. I'm sorry I didn't mention it before, but I didn't know if your story had anything to do with antiques.'

'No, there was no way you could have known. We were trying to keep it quiet,' Steve said.

'I keep all the old papers for getting the fire started in the winter. If you come back in, we can probably find the editions that carried the story.'

They followed her back into the house and through the kitchen and into the little utility room, next to the coal house. A neatly stacked pile of newspapers lay on a low shelf next to the washing machine. Iris picked a handful off the top of the pile and laid them onto the washing machine. She quickly shuffled through them and pulled out three papers and handed them to Steve.

'That's all there has been I think,' Iris said. 'I remember thinking how quickly stories lose their interest. When it happened everyone in the town was shocked and, I think, frightened. I know I was. But when nothing happens, and no one is arrested, life just goes back to normal. I didn't know him, but it is a terrible thing to happen, especially in a small town like this.'

'It's a good thing that you mentioned this,' Emily said. 'We will read these carefully and see if our investigations can help in this case too.'

'Yes, you've given us a good start with these,' Steve said. 'This murder may have no link to our story, but I have a feeling it has.'

As promised when they arrived at the Hotel de Paris, they were shown to a lovely room at the front, overlooking the pier and promenade.

'Did you see mother blush when she talked about the manager here?' Steve asked Emily.

'Yes,' she said, 'I detect romance in the air. And good for her.'

'I think she said he was Italian when I spoke to her yesterday,' Steve said.

'Well, judging by the room he has given us, he is a very nice man.'

After they unpacked, they read through the newspapers that Iris had given them. It sounded like a particularly gruesome attack. The police seemed to be looking for local thugs who may have been interrupted in the middle of an attempted burglary and panicked. For the rest of the story the local journalist, starved of any other information, had done a pretty good job of mentioning almost everything else that might have been a motive. These ranged from the burglary gone wrong theory to someone looking for an extremely rare and valuable item or a vendetta involving another dealer.

'I think we will try and contact Eric tomorrow,' said Steve. 'He knows a lot of people in the town, and I am sure he will have a theory on what happened and maybe give us a few pointers to the man we're are looking for.'

CHAPTER 5

Elizabeth Naylor, or Lizzie as she preferred to be called, woke to hear the front door close. Micky was on his way to London. Since her depression, they had slept in separate rooms by mutual consent. And that is how it continued when they came to Norfolk. She got out of her bed and ran to the window to see Micky driving his big Jag out onto the road. Good, she thought, I will get up now.

Micky had insisted they brought with them the huge double bed that they had in London, even though the bedroom here was barely large enough. The en-suite and large dressing room had been added to the house some years before they had moved to Cromer. When they got there, Micky tried to persuade her to share the big bed again, but she said that she still did not sleep well and didn't want to keep him awake all night.

Lizzie liked Cromer, even though she resisted the idea at first. She had lived all her life in London, and the thought of being that far away from the excitement of a big city filled her with dread.

It was made worse by her realisation that she had made a big mistake when she ignored the pleadings of her parents and married Micky. She was swept off her feet by the flashy man who was full of confidence, free with his money and welcomed wherever he went in London. Lizzie had the looks and the breeding to be the ideal girl for Micky, to complete the image of a highly successful businessman. And she loved it when she and Micky were photographed arriving at a film premiere or at a party to launch yet another new rock band.

Her father had simply said in his rather old-fashioned military way 'I don't like him because the man is a crook, and I don't want my daughter seen out and about with the likes of him.'

She told him that the world was changing and that many people like Micky were going to change society completely. 'Lots of people are now setting the trends and making fortunes,' she added.

'I don't mind singers, actors, fashion designers and people like that making money, they earn it, but that man is a crook,' he said. 'And he is too old for you. He is old enough to be your father,' he added.

'Well he doesn't look old, and that's all that really matters.' She countered.

Lizzie, of course, did not believe her father and left home. She was twenty-one then, and six months later they married at a registry office in Greenwich. For a couple of years, she was happy enough with their lifestyle and still believed that Micky was a successful dealer in antique jewellery.

She began to think that things were not as they should be when the police began to call and spend time talking to Micky. Then on one occasion, they took him off to the police station, and he was gone for several hours.

When he came back, he was strangely subdued for several days. Soon afterwards, he announced that they were going to move to Norfolk. Lizzie said that she was not going to leave London under any circumstances. That brought on a huge row, with Micky screaming and shouting at her in a way that she still could not believe. For days, it was as if she was shell-shocked. She hardly dare say anything for fear of triggering another outburst. She could not sleep or eat and did not want to go out, even to go shopping.

She went to see her doctor, and he said she was depressed. He prescribed some tablets, but they did not help. She felt that she was walking through a very dark tunnel and there was no light at the end. She was hardly eating and did not want to go anywhere or talk to anyone.

When the time came to move, she didn't have the energy to do anything to help. Micky hired a removal company that packed everything and unpacked it all when they arrived. Micky was hardly speaking to her, and the journey from London to Cromer was largely silent.

Then, as they began to near the coast, a strange feeling came over her. She felt her spirits begin to lift. It was a strange feeling, and she almost felt like laughing. She had come out of the dark tunnel into the sunlight. She suddenly didn't care what Micky said to her. She could start a new life here.

Euphoria had taken over, and she felt happy for the first time in many months. When they reached the house; it too, was love at first sight. It was a lovely white house, set on top of the cliffs, with large windows overlooking the sea. The garden was lovely, and there was a pool.

She brought herself back quickly from memories of those dark days. She had learned to live with Micky's deceit and lies. If he could live a secret life, so would she. She would put up with his constant trips back to London to see old girlfriends or more likely new prostitutes.

She knew this because when business was involved, the people who were now running things for him in London had to come to see him. But he still made his trips to London, 'to make sure nobody was ripping him off,' he used to say. As if any of them dare risk that, thought Lizzie.

So, she had her own secret life, together with the half-truths and deception that go with it. Did Micky know about her new life? She didn't know or care really. The only thing she did know was that she was never going to allow him to push her back into those weeks of depression. Now she had time to think about what had happened, the thing that really hurt her was that she had believed Micky ran an honest, legitimate business. She believed all his lies, and she did not believe her father. Now she was estranged from her mother, father and sister. Micky had taken all that away from her, and she hated him for what he had done.

CHAPTER 6

Micky had taken an early train from Cromer and reached Norwich at around 9.30 in the morning and was now sitting in a private meeting room he rented at a hotel close to Norwich train station.

He had woken early, showered and left the house while Lizzie was still asleep, or more likely pretending to be asleep until he went out of the door. It was better that way, even though she had given up asking him where he was going and what he was doing.

In fairness, she had been a lot better since they moved to Cromer, which was strange considering the song and dance and moaning and groaning that went on when he told her that they were coming to Norfolk. She said she had depression. What had she got to be depressed about? She had all the money she wanted, designer clothes, they went to the best parties in town and got to know the top people. He decided that he would never understand women.

Things suited him as they were now. He could get all the girls he wanted back in London. That was why he had set himself up with a nice little apartment on the Edgeware Road. It was a pleasant, discrete place, not far for the girls to travel and it kept him out of sight from any rozzers that might be on the prowl.

He often wondered if Lizzie knew what he was doing in London. One of these days he would tell her and enjoy the look on her face when he did. But, at the moment, she was still very useful to him. She gave him respectability, with her father being a big-shot Army man and her public-school education. And she was still a real looker despite her being a miserable pain in the arse most of the time. He wouldn't rock the boat at present; there were too many other things going on.

The door of the meeting room opened, and Guus Visser walked in, followed by a waitress with a tray of coffee and biscuits. Micky stood up and greeted Guus with a warm handshake. They sat down in the two large, comfortable chairs and waited for the waitress to finish shuffling the cups and plates around. Micky was a little anxious as to why Guus had called this meeting at such short notice, but he would not ask. That would just show that he was concerned.

Guus looked like everyone's favourite grandfather. He was a smallish man, with silver grey hair, round face and wire-framed glasses that made his eyes look large, giving him a permanent look of surprise. Micky had known Guus for almost twenty years now. They met in Berlin, soon after the end of the war. Guus had a different name then, and Micky was never sure what nationality he was.

To Micky, he was simply known as Victor. At the time, Micky thought he might be Polish or Ukrainian or even Russian. Berlin at that time was a city in turmoil. Looting, murder and rape were commonplace, and the city was virtually run by the gangs of black-marketeers. These were mostly American forces who had the goods to sell, and the main buyers were the Russians, who, having not been paid for the last three months of the war, were given full back pay and told they had to spend it in Berlin.

Micky and his mate were in an army transport division and were part of a big operation to get food supplies to Berlin for the local population, who suddenly found themselves with no food, hardly any water and very little housing left intact. Victor had suggested to Micky that if they delivered two-thirds of the supplies to where they were supposed to go, he would sell the rest on the black market, making good profits, which they would then share. Micky was doubtful at first, but when the money came rolling in, and with no real risks, they soon found themselves looking for places to hide the money.

Victor was the supreme organiser. He had people working for him all over Berlin. Many different nationalities, working in small cells, without any one gang knowing who the others were. All he asked was efficiency and honesty. If he didn't get it, you were finished. He never raised his voice to anyone, but no one could cross him and get away with it.

Years later, he made contact with Micky again. This time with a project for peacetime, which required a little more subtlety, than those during the chaos of wartime. But the rewards were even better.

After making a great play of pouring the coffee, adding the milk and two lumps of sugar in Micky's, Guus sat back in the armchair and fixed Micky with his magnified blue eyes.

'So, Micky, how are things with you?' he asked in a near perfect English accent.

'Pretty good, yes pretty good.' Micky nodded nervously, still worrying about why Guus had called the meeting.

'Are you finding that running the business from here is causing any problems?'

'No, no problems. It's working well. Most of the time the boys come up here to see me, but occasionally I go to town to make sure that everything is okay. You know, keep them on their toes.' Micky was beginning think that he had worried unnecessarily.

'And the quality of the things that we are sending to you? Is the quality good? Are the prices we are setting allowing you to get a good margin?' he asked, with a rare smile.

'Oh yes. The items are very high quality, and we are getting good margins,' said Micky.

'That is how it should be, we are fair to each other and trust each other, and we are both happy. This is why I approached you in the first place; it gets over a major problem from which we were both suffering. High-quality items stolen in the UK run the risk of being recognised. High-quality items stolen in the Netherlands or Belgium or even France might also be recognised in those countries. So, the simple solution is to send my stolen items to you and for to send yours to me. It works, does it not, it works perfectly.'

'Absolutely,' said Micky. 'It was a brilliant idea.'

Guus leant forward in his chair. 'Yes, it works as long as we don't draw attention to ourselves with stupidity. I had to warn you about your flashy lifestyle in London. You ignored my advice and then the police started to take notice and harass you. You took my advice and moved away from where your teams are operating. As you just explained to me, that seemed to be working well. No?'

'Yes,' said Micky quietly. 'He was beginning to see which way this conversation was going.'

'You have been keeping a low profile, here on the coast?'

'Well, yes but…'

Guus cut him short. 'Then why, in a small town, with hardly any crime at all, is an antique dealer murdered in his shop.'

'How did you know about that? It wasn't anything to do with me.'

'With a business partnership like ours, I cannot afford not to know what is going on. Of course, I knew. Now I want an explanation of what *is* going on. Why did you find it necessary to kill that man? Had he been threatening you?'

'Yes, he was, in a way. He kept saying that I was a dodgy dealer, up to no good and probably dealing in stolen goods.'

'As I heard it, he is one of those people who dislikes strangers moving into the town and particularly the ones who seem to have plenty of money. Apparently, the locals all know what he is like and ignore him now. They say he is just jealous of anyone who seems to be doing better than he is. In other words, he was a harmless idiot.'

'I thought people might start believing what he was saying,' Micky mumbled almost to himself.

'Okay, so he was saying bad things about you. Is that a good reason to kill him and bring the police into it.'

'It wasn't what I intended. I told Arthur and Shay to give him a scare, put the wind up him so he would keep his mouth shut. They got into his shop and lured him downstairs, but he came down with a baseball bat and caught Arthur with a couple of heavy blows to the head. Shay pulled the guy away from Arthur, who I think was concussed after the two clouts with the bat. Arthur just got up and charged straight at the shopkeeper. The knife went straight in and killed him.'

Guus stared at Micky for several minutes, and then said, 'this has got to stop Micky. It just won't do. Trouble seems to be following you around, and you must do something about it and quickly. Arthur has got to be taken out of this altogether. He is a liability. Speak to Shay, explain the situation and tell him to take Arthur well away from here and make sure he is not found. You understand?

'In this part of the world you do not need any more muscle than one good man, and I know Shay is good. Then you must make an effort to be part of the community. Give some money to good causes, go into pubs and talk to the locals. This is not London. You can't be an unseen stranger here. Get that lovely wife of yours to play her part too; she is a very nice young woman. She will help you, won't she?'

'Yes, Lizzie will help alright,' Micky said without thinking. He was so relieved that Guus was making positive suggestions about the future, when just a few minutes before, Micky feared the worst.

Guus abruptly stood up and shook hands with Micky. 'I shall leave now, simply because I think that you have a great deal to do to make things right. Please do exactly as I have suggested, and if it works out well, things can be quickly back to normal. We will let business carry on because we are committed to many people and we don't want to cause a storm or let anyone down. The routes we use are not compromised, our couriers are not compromised, it is you who is in danger of being compromised Micky, and that just will not do.'

He turned towards the door and then said, without turning around to face Micky, 'This is your last chance, Micky. I cannot let this go on any further.'

CHAPTER 7

Emily and Steve arranged to meet Eric, an old school friend of Steve's, at a pub in Sheringham. Eric was very bright, and he and Steve used to compete with one another to get the best marks in their class. It was always neck and neck in their improvised race, but no matter who won they stayed firm friends. When the time came to leave school and choose a career, Steve chose journalism, which began on the local paper, but it would inevitably take him away from his hometown.

Eric hated the thought of having to leave Cromer and decided to take a plumbing apprenticeship with a small local company. He was always the more practical person, and he loved the job. His reasons for wanting to stay in Cromer was strongly influenced by Carol, a very pretty, dark-haired girl, with whom Eric was infatuated. Before the first year of his apprenticeship, they had broken up, but Eric still did not regret his decision to stay in the town.

Steve and Emily sat quietly together in the corner of the lounge. As they waited for Eric, Steve ran through the story of Eric's life so far.

'There have been numerous girls since Carol, some have lasted a couple of years, others just a couple of weeks,' Steve said. 'Eric is constantly worried about making the wrong choice when it comes to any commitment. If there is, perhaps, just some little thing that he doesn't like, he concentrates solely on that, forgetting all the good things.'

'I take it he doesn't understand that people change as well,' Emily said.

'Exactly. He is a good guy and a great friend, but when it comes to the give and take of a relationship, he's like a stubborn old mule.'

The pub they had chosen for their meeting was a new red brick building on the outskirts of the town. It was a place for locals, rather than holidaymakers and there was no one else in the lounge, which was the main reason for choosing it.

Eric came in and immediately walked over to where Emily and Steve were sitting. He greeted Steve and shook hands with Emily.

'What do you want to drink?' Eric asked. He was slightly shorter than Steve, and a much stockier build.

'No, you are doing us a favour Eric, and besides, this is on expenses, so the drinks and lunch are on us.'

After the beer and sandwiches arrived, they settled down to talk. To start with, Steve wanted to know what was happening in Eric's life and learnt that Susan was the current love of his life and that Eric's boss had decided to retire, and had sold the business to Eric. He got a loan from the bank to buy it, and business was good. There was a big change going on with hotels and B&Bs wanting to install ensuite facilities. Susan was also praised because she was good at looking after his accounts.

'You always were an old romantic Eric,' Steve said. Eric pretended not to know what Emily and Steve were laughing about.

'Thanks for meeting with us,' Steve said, 'sorry it had to be a bit cloak and dagger.'

Eric grinned, 'Yes, I wondered what it was all about – meeting where we weren't likely to be overheard and where nobody was likely to recognise us.'

'Yes, I know,' Steve laughed, 'but it is important. And I don't want you to get involved before you know what it's all about.'

'Okay, tell me,' he said taking a drink from his glass.

'We came here to investigate a tip-off that a big-time London crook has moved up here because the police in London were giving him a hard time. He must have thought the quietness and isolation of North Norfolk was what he needed, while continuing to run his operations in London,' Steve paused to see if he got any reaction from Eric.

Eric nodded. 'Yes, I have heard that said, but I didn't believe it. You know the yarns that you get told in the pubs in Cromer. Particularly those near the front. The locals just love to wind up the holidaymakers who come in for a drink or two and a bit of local colour. I heard one of the crab fishermen telling a townie that he had once seen a ghost ship sailing across a sandbank just off Blakeney Point. He said the ship's sails were all set and you could hear the cries of those on board as it was swept out to sea. The man was well loaded with the local brew and just kept saying 'and what happened next' every time the story seemed to be ending. He didn't seem to notice everybody else in the pub falling about laughing. Well, that's how I took the gangster story, with a pinch of salt.'

'Yes, I don't blame you,' said Steve. 'We had our doubts, but when we went to see my mother, she went to ask her next-door neighbour, who I understand has a degree in nosiness, and she said she knew someone who fitted the description.'

'Who's that?' asked Eric, his voice full of disbelief.

Emily said, having looked quickly around the room to make sure they were still alone. 'His name is Micky, he has a very pretty wife, and they live in a big house on Cliff Drive.'

Eric nodded. 'Yes, I know who you mean, they are a flashy pair, he drives a big Jag. As far as I was concerned, he was just a youngish bloke with plenty of money. Let's face it there are plenty of them around these days. I didn't like the look of him, but I had no reason to believe that he was dodgy.'

'When you are in the pub,' said Steve, 'could you bring the subject of Micky up and find out what other people think. Be non-committal about what you think, because there is a chance that if you say too much about him, he is likely to silence you for good.

Eric went white. 'Christ, you don't think that's what happened to Morris Barnack do you?'

'It is possible,' Emily said. 'That is why we are so careful, and you must take care as well. If there is anyone in the bar that you don't know, don't bring the subject up. We will find out another way.'

'Well, I didn't expect that,' Eric said, still a little pale. 'I usually drop in for one on the way home. That's how I pick up most of my work. People go to the pub for a pint, talk about what they want to do with home improvements. The Landlord of the pub gets their names and addresses, and I go around and give them a quote. There is a builder, an electrician and a gardener who also go there in the early evening to pick up any enquiries. They would certainly notice any strangers in town.'

'That sounds good, but keep it low key, we don't want to start a panic.' said Steve. 'When do you think we can meet up again?'

'I'll ring your mum,' said Eric. 'I haven't had a chat with her for a while.'

'Okay, but don't tell her what you have found out. She'll be digging out the deerstalker and magnifying glass and going off in search of clues.' Steve said with a laugh.

'No, I won't say a word, and I'll pick a place to meet that is safe.'

'Yes, that will be good,' Emily said, 'but when this is all over, and we are ready to go home we want to meet Susan.'

'Yes, that would be great,' Eric said, standing up and holding onto his sandwich. 'I've got to go now, I've left my apprentice trying to fit some bath taps, so the chances are the house is flooded now.' He rushed out the door with a mouthful of cheese and ham sandwich.

'Do you think he will be all right?' Emily asked Steve.

'Yes, Eric is one of the most reliable people I know. He absorbs information in seconds and works out what he is going to do almost as quickly. I would say he's wasted being a plumber, but you can't blame him for not wanting to leave a place like this and I bet you wouldn't find a better plumber anywhere. And now he's found Susan his accounts will be perfect as well.

CHAPTER 8

The police station probably looked the same as it did fifty years ago. Well-scrubbed wooden flooring, the walls were painted white, and the partitions between rooms was a golden, varnished wood. There was a small waiting area, with what looked like a row of old school chairs laid out in a long line. A young woman and small boy occupied two of the chairs. They faced a desk, behind which a police officer stood, leaning forward over an open ledger. He was writing in it with painstaking care and appearing not to notice that there was anyone else in the room. Beyond the desk were some small offices, divided by the varnished wood and glass partitions.

Emily and Steve stepped inside and hesitated. The policeman at the desk did not look up, so they looked towards the woman and small boy, to discover if there was a queue. They both looked away, so Emily and Steve went and sat down right at the opposite end of the row of chairs. The man at the desk continued to write in his book, and the woman and boy sat in silence looking at each other.

Emily and Steve had discussed whether they should come to the police station and ask about the murder of Morris Barnack. In the end, they decided that they would give it a try, but were not expecting to be told anything that they had not already seen in the newspapers.

'Do you think we are wasting our time?' Emily whispered.

In reply, Steve just nodded.

The policeman at the desk looked up at them and then went back to his writing. Steve decided to make a move and signalled Emily to follow him. He walked over to the desk, took his press card out of his pocket and placed it on the desk in front of the officer.

The policeman, who looked quite elderly, had a purple bulbous nose and bushy grey eyebrows. He picked up the card and studied it and then looked at Emily. She produced her press card from her handbag and gave it to the officer.

He handed the cards back to them and said, 'What do you want?'

'We've come up from London to find out how the investigation into the murder of the antique dealer is progressing.' Steve said, with great authority.

'Who are you working for?'

'Daily Mail,' Steve answered, thinking that the Constable would probably not be a reader of Inside London.

The officer rubbed and squeezed his nose as he thought what to do next. 'I can't talk to the press. You'll have to make an appointment,' he said, trying to go back to his writing.

'Who with?' ask Emily.

He looked flustered and snapped, 'With the Sergeant, he's in charge.'

'Look,' said Steve, adopting his let's be sensible voice. 'We are on very tight deadlines and need to get a story quickly. Either your Sergeant can update us on how the investigation is going, or we will have to go around the town talking to the local people and then present it as their opinion of the investigation's progress.'

'And from what we have heard so far,' Emily added, 'the answer is nowhere.'

There was more rubbing of his nose. He looked over at the woman and child, and they were staring at the three of them standing at the desk.

'Just wait here, I'll go and get the Sergeant.' He turned and plodded across the room and disappeared to somewhere at the back of the station. In a surprisingly short time, he was back.

'If you come through, the Sergeant will speak to you. It's the door on the left,' he waved a hand towards the back of a corridor and went back to his ledger.

The Sergeant was younger than they had expected. He stood up as soon as they entered the office and shook hands with them both. He introduced himself as Sergeant Brian Brooks and asked them to sit down. Emily and Steve were fascinated by the contrast between the desk Constable and the smiling, courteousness of Brian Brooks.

Emily was the first to recover from the surprise. 'Thank you for seeing us,' she said, 'we know you must be very busy but, we would like to get an update on the investigation into the murder of Morris Barnack.'

'Yes, of course,' Brooks said, 'but I am a little surprised that a murder in Cromer would be of any interest to the newspapers in London.'

'National newspapers and magazines will always be interested in a grisly murder in a quiet seaside town,' she said.

Brooks nodded his understanding. 'I quite understand, but I am afraid that there has been very little progress. We are relatively certain that the attack was a burglary that went wrong. We think two men broke in with the intention of stealing some of the expensive antique jewellery that was on display in several locked cabinets.'

'Are there any suspects?' Emily asked.

'No, we are almost certain that these were strangers to the town. With the improvement to roads in recent years it has become easy for people to drive here from Norwich, Kings Lynn or Peterborough, or even further afield like Birmingham, carry out the burglary and be miles away before the crime has been discovered,' Brooks said.

'What makes you so certain that it wasn't someone local?' Emily asked.

'Well, to start with we would have heard something. This is a close-knit community and we, the local police, are part of that community. We would have heard something. And secondly, I am a strong believer in statistics, and from my own experience the most likely perpetrators are people from outside the town.'

'So, what happens now?' Steve asked.

'The enquiry goes on, and we're working with police throughout the region to catch the people who committed this dreadful crime.'

Emily and Steve walked to the car park two streets away, where they had parked the Spitfire. Neither of them spoke until they got into the car.

'What was all that nonsense about?' Steve said.

'I think he was making it up as he went along,' Emily said. 'He is doing absolutely nothing about it. He is just waiting for it to be forgotten.'

'The question is?' said Steve. 'Is he stupid or is he bent.'

'Well, I certainly don't think he's stupid. The trouble is he must think we are,' she said.

'Exactly, why didn't he just say, 'No comment' and send us on our way or refer us to a spokesman at headquarters? That would be the normal response and the one I expected. That's what the man on the desk expected. But no, we were invited in to hear a load of old waffle. He has something to hide and in his anxiety to cover it up he has just made us more suspicious.'

CHAPTER 9

Lizzie had thought that Micky was going away for a couple of days and she got up early so that she could make the best of the day. But he spoilt her happiness by saying that his plans had changed and he had people to talk to in Cromer. Fortunately, Will, some weeks before, had the foresight to work out an alternative plan if anything cropped up unexpectedly.

If Lizzie or Will got delayed and could not get to their normal meeting place near the pier, they would go to plan B. This meant a short walk along the beach in the direction of Overstrand, a small village just along the coast. When they reached the last line of beach huts, they continued until they reached the hut at the end. It had belonged to Will's family for many years, although he was the only one who used it now. Being last in the line gave it a privacy that the other beach huts did not enjoy, and it also allowed a good view of the beach in either direction.

Will treasured this convenient little hideaway. He was a good-looking young man, in a rough and rugged way, and he had an immediate attraction for the girls who had come on holiday with their parents and were finding Cromer less exciting than they had expected.

They would come down to the beach in front of the lifeboat station and watch the crab boats come in. Most of the boats were worked by men approaching their senior years or at least they seemed that to teenage girls. It wasn't a particularly attractive life for the young men of the town, so many of them looked elsewhere for work.

Will, however, loved everything about it. The fresh air, the constant battle with the sea, the camaraderie amongst the fishermen. And, most of all, he loved the attention he got when the girls pressed forward to look in his boat. Will also knew just how to play the audience. He never looked at the girls; he would always direct his friendly smile to the parents, or little brother, grandad or grandma.

He knew the girls would come back when the rest of the family were tired of looking at crabs and had moved on to build sand castles or play cricket on the beach. Sometimes the young ones would come back, for another look at Will, but when they saw that he wasn't interested, they would melt away.

But there was usually one, in their late teens or early 20's, who was still living at home, and maybe mum and dad put their foot down and said she wasn't going to stay at home alone. It was usually because some unwelcome young man was hanging around their daughter, and they just wanted to get her away from him.

These girls made an instant connection with Will. He was only a couple of years older than they were and he understood how they were feeling. They were grown-up young women, perfectly able to make their own decisions, and Will was going to give them a good time while they were on holiday. And a good time they had. He would take them straight to the beach hut nestling under the cliffs. He kept the beach hut clean and tidy. Will painted it inside and out every spring. There were two deck chairs if they wanted to sunbathe, a table and two comfortable chairs, and a sofa bed. The drinks cupboard was well stocked with beer, Babycham and crisps, plus a drawer full of rubber Johnnies. Will believed in safety first with his pleasures, and it was only fair to the girls.

But then Lizzie came along, and his life had changed forever. She came down to look in his boat one cold morning in early June. Will had looked up and there in front of him was the most beautiful woman he had ever seen. He sat there, in amongst the mess of crab pots, boxes and rope, his mouth hanging open like an idiot. He couldn't even manage a smile.

'Good catch today?' she asked. Will detected what he would call a posh voice, but it was soft and light and, he thought, had a slight hint of sadness.

'Yes,' he said, and then remembered that it was a terrible catch. He looked down at the pathetic few crabs in the box between his feet. 'Well no, it's actually pathetic.'

She laughed, and this time her voice sounded as beautiful as she looked.

She sat on the edge of his boat, and they talked while he worked and afterwards she asked if he would like to go and have a drink with her. He knew he should say no. This was all wrong. He was the one who should be in charge of seduction, not her. But why not, he asked himself? What had he got to lose?

Her car was parked at the top of The Gangway, the short-cobbled road that runs steeply down to the beach. She expertly turned the car around at the top of the hill and drove quickly through the streets and out along the Holt road. She was wearing a smart, red trouser suit, which went wonderfully with her black hair. He was still dressed in the trousers and a navy sweater that he wore under his oilskins.

'Where are we going?' he asked, doing his best to suppress his Norfolk accent.

'To a pub in Holt,' she said.

'I can't go like this and sit in in a pub.'

'Don't worry; we will sit in the garden at the back. People wear all sort of things outside.'

Lizzie insisted on buying the drinks, and they took them into the backyard of the pub, which they grandly called the Beer Garden. Will knew this was all wrong. He was being swept along without any idea where this would end. Lizzie was probably only a year or so older than him, but he felt like an awkward teen.

He remembered two of the old hands on the crab boats playing a trick on him once. He was a gullible young lad, just starting out on the boats. They challenged him to a race down the Gangway, the steep cobbled street that leads down to the beach. First on the beach would be the winner. They called ready, steady, go and Will set off at a fine pace, but quickly realised he was the only one in the race and stopping was going to be a big problem. In an absolute panic, he saw a large tarpaulin laying folded at the side on the road. He swerved towards the tarpaulin flung himself onto it. He did a couple of somersaults into a pile of rope crab pots. He picked himself up and extracted himself from the pots, with the laughter from the two challengers at the top of The Gangway, drowned by the hilarity of those who had been eagerly watching the event from the beach.

Will was shaken, but as always, he saw the funny side of it and laughed at what a fool he had made of himself. That was what made him so popular with the older fishermen. Will was always ready to see the funny side of life, but this first encounter with Lizzie felt as if he was running downhill again, and there was nothing to stop him this time. It was way beyond his understanding.

The situation very quickly became clear to Will. Lizzie was completely open with him. She said she was married and that she had now discovered that her husband was a crook. She had believed that he was a successful businessman when she had married him. She said she still wasn't certain what his so-called business was, but she knew that he was a liar and a cheat and would stop at nothing to get his way.

She told Will how he had treated her, about her months of depression and him constantly going to London to see girlfriends and prostitutes. He didn't even bother to deny it anymore.

'I woke up one-day last week and decided that I was going to have a life of my own. He tricked me into marrying him and then didn't care at all when I was so devastated. He has replaced me with his women in London, but he still needs me to give him respectability in Cromer. I'm scared of what he might do if I left him or asked for a divorce, but I don't see why I shouldn't have a life.'

'What makes you think I can make you happy?' Will asked.

She laughed. 'I was just wandering around this morning, thinking how I could make my life better and, as if by magic, I saw this handsome young man, sitting in his boat and looking content with life. We talked, and I felt we were both happy.'

'Yes,' said Will, 'it's surprising how happy I can look with a catch of six crabs.'

She laughed. 'Well, you looked happy to me.'

That's how it all started for Lizzie and Will. She had felt extraordinarily bold going out and picking up a man like that, but Will was such an easy-going sort of person that it all seemed quite natural.

Will was not quite so forthcoming with information about his life before they met. He admitted to one or two affairs with girls on holiday, but he thought it best not to boast to Lizzie of his conquests, the way that he did to the other fishermen. In fact, he had been guilty of some enhancement of his stories, which had built his reputation as a stud to near legendary proportions.

But as far as Lizzie was concerned, it was just a handful of holiday romances, that meant little to either him or the girls. But he had confessed to where these acts of fleeting pleasure had taken place and, consequentially, it was chosen as the go-to place when their normal meetings failed for one reason or another.

In fact, it had never been needed until today. They had always met on time and driven to the little cottage at Salthouse. Lizzie rented it at present but planned to buy it for her new life. But today, Will was left waiting on the beach, near the pier.

He waited until the normal meeting time and then wandered slowly towards the beach hut, idly playing ducks and drakes with any smooth, flat stones he saw as he walked. He reached the hut and sat himself down on the steps that led up to the door.

It was a pleasantly warm September afternoon, with a gentle cooling breeze. Will began to feel warm, so he unlocked the hut and took a bottle of beer from the cupboard at the back of the hut, which was usually in the shade. The bottle felt nice and cool. He sat down on the steps again so that Lizzie would see him when she came along.

It was only about half an hour that he had to wait and he would have happily waited all day. There was Lizzie in a short, pink mini skirt and matching top, walking along the sand on the edge of the sea, carrying pair of flip-flops.

She waved at Will, and after checking that there was no one following her, he jumped up and ran to meet her. They kissed briefly, and a little nervously, both of them realising that when they were out in the open, anyone might be watching them. They hurried to the hut, and inside they kissed again.

'This is lovely,' said Lizzie excitedly. 'On a day like today, it's better than the cottage. Your little seduction den. I wish we had tried this before.'

She took her skirt and top off, to reveal a tiny white bikini. 'I might as well get a little sun.' She sat down on the steps.

'The drinks cupboard is stocked, but the choice is limited' he said. 'Beer or Babycham?'

She chose a beer, and he sat down next to her.

'You didn't ask why I was late?' she said.

'I worried a bit, but when I saw you walking along the sand, looking happy, I thought it couldn't have been anything really bad. You are here with me, and that's all that matters.'

She smiled and said, 'I do love you Will.' He gently touched her naked back.

'Micky was due to go to London for two days, to see his women no doubt. But he said something had cropped up, and he needed to stay in Cromer. Meeting someone he said, but I don't believe anything he says anymore.'

Will didn't care what Micky was doing. He must be a complete idiot to treat a girl like Lizzie so badly.

'Come on,' she said, standing up and walking into the beach hut. 'Make another holiday girl very happy.'

They made love and then just lay naked and contented together on the sofa bed.

The crunch of footsteps along the pebble beach and the panting of a dog pulling on his lead only served to send Lizzie into a fit of giggling.

For a while, they just lay there and talked in a whisper.

'There is something I have meant to ask you,' Lizzie said. 'When I walk past you, and you are working on the boat, and I hear you talking to the other fishermen, I can't understand a word you say. But when you are with me I understand everything.'

'It's the Norfolk accent. A lot of the words we use are completely different from English. And you're not meant to understand it. That way we can talk about the visitors without them knowing. We are multi-lingual in Cromer,' he laughed.

'And stop asking difficult questions,' he said, 'you'll make my brain hurt.'

He reached over and began to stroke her again. He looked at her beautiful tanned body and the tiny white lines left by the bikini. He rolled gently on top of her and felt her soft skin against his body. They kissed, and she held him close to her. He had never seen her as happy as this.'

'You love the excitement of making love here, don't you?'

'I love the excitement of making love with you anywhere,' she replied.

'But particularly here, on the beach.'

'Yes I do,' she whispered, and they made love again.

CHAPTER 10

Micky was at home in his office when Lizzie came back late in the afternoon. She came in and went straight up to her room. He was going to ask her why she was walking around in that little bloody mini skirt that showed everything, but he was glad he didn't. He had a lot on his mind and could do without having another bloody row with her. He suspected she was fucking somebody else, but right at this moment, he couldn't care less.

When all the current mess was cleared up, then he could start to sort things out with her. The ungrateful bitch had caused him more than enough trouble, both before and after they moved to Norfolk. He thought she would go and find someone after she had accused him of visiting girlfriends and prostitutes in London. It was none of her damn business what he did in London, so he hadn't even bothered to deny it.

He would get everything sorted out so that Guus Visser was happy again and then he would find out what she had been up to and she would pay the price for cheating on him. And so would whoever she had been fucking.

The following day Lizzie was still in bed when Micky left the house. He drove round to the house where Arthur and Shay live. It was a small semi-detached house that Micky had bought to unload some spare cash. It was a miserable little place, but they didn't complain because they got plenty of trips down to London, or civilisation, as they like to call it.

Shay was up and ready to go when Micky arrived.

'Where's Arthur?' Micky asked.

'Still asleep I should think, it's only half past six.'

'Well, tell the lazy bastard to get up. I've got a job for him and it's urgent.'

'Is it a job for me as well?' Shay asked.

'No, I've got something else for you. I'll tell you about it after he's gone.'

'I thought we were always supposed to work together so that I could keep an eye on him.'

'This is a straightforward job. Taking a cheque in a sealed envelope to a man in Peterborough and then bringing back a small parcel. Nothing he can do wrong. Just go and bloody well tell him to get his arse down here and stop giving me a hard time.'

'Okay, okay,' said Shay and bellowed the message up the stairs.

'So, everything's all right, is it?' asked Shay, sensing that something wasn't.

'No, it's not bloody all right. The Dutchman's on the warpath about the waves we have been creating here.'

'What waves,' said Shay, trying to look innocent.

'A dead fucking antique dealer. That is what is bothering him and me. Had you forgotten that you and Arthur managed to kill the poor bastard? Had it slipped your memory?'

Fortunately, a dishevelled Arthur arrived at that moment, looking alarmed at the raised voices.

Micky immediately toned his voice down. The last thing he wanted to do was to put the wind up Arthur. He knew very well who cocked up at the antique dealer's shop. They had to let him think that they would straighten things out with the police and they had. And now it suited Micky to let Arthur think that everything had been put right.

Micky gave him the sealed envelope with a handwritten address on the front. He told him to take it to that address, deliver it and then go back two hours later and pick up a box with valuable stuff in it, so he had to keep it safe.

Arthur nodded his understanding and then asked if Shay was coming with him.

'No Arthur, I have got another job for Shay,' Micky cut in. 'We are busy, so you take that and look after your job, and Shay will look after his job.'

Arthur still didn't look particularly happy with the arrangement, but he got himself together and went.

As soon as his car disappeared down the road, Micky turned to Shay. 'We'd better go and sit down while I tell you what we have to do.'

They walked through to the meagre little kitchen and sat down at the table. Shay spooned instant coffee into two cups and added hot water from the kettle.

Micky looked tired and stressed and sat stirring his coffee.

'So, what have we got to do?' Shay asked because it didn't look as though Micky was ever going to tell him.

'The Dutchman says we've got to get rid of Arthur.'

'What, sack him?' Shay said in surprise.

'No, for Christ sake. Top him, kill him, and get rid of the body. He says he is a liability and if we don't do it, he will bring his people in to do it and that would be curtains for you and me as well.'

'Did he say that?' Shay asked.

'No, but I know how Guus works. I knew him when his name wasn't Guus, and he wasn't Dutch. I worked with him in Berlin, 1946. He is a ruthless bastard. If things are going well, he is the nicest guy you could meet, but if they go wrong, he'll take no chances at all.

'Arthur has to go, and we have got to take care of it. It makes sense when you think about it. Arthur is a useless tool, but he knows too much about the way we run things. He's got to go, and we have to do it soon.'

Shay sat thinking for a few minutes and then said, 'Yeah, no matter how you look at it, it's the only way. We'll have to work something out.'

'Yes, and bloody quick too. I am certain Guus has someone over here, in Cromer, working for him. When I met him a couple of days ago, he knew everything that was going on, even what the local gossips were saying. That's what shook me. He even tested me out about Lizzie, asking if she would support me in getting on the right side of the big nobs in the town. I don't know why he said that. Have you heard anything about Lizzie? Is she fucking someone behind my back?'

'No, of course, she's not. Lizzie wouldn't do anything like that.'

'You don't know her,' Micky said. 'She can be a spiteful bitch.'

Shay didn't reply. He wasn't about to get drawn into bad-mouthing Lizzie. He had always liked her and knew that Micky had treated her badly. They sat in silence, both with their thoughts.

'Can you think of anyone, close to the business, who might be reporting back to Guus?'

'No, but it needn't be someone close to the business, 'said Shay. 'Guus runs it, Guus put the structure in place, Guus knows it better than we do. All he needs is someone to listen to the gossip in the pubs and on the street, he knows the rest.'

'Yes, you're right.' Micky suddenly brightened up. 'That's a relief. I didn't want to have to go around trying to figure out who it was and even if I knew I couldn't do anything about it.

'Let's think about how we can handle this business with Arthur,' Micky said.

'Are you sure there's no other way? I'll agree that Arthur is not the brightest tool in the box, and he can be a complete prat, but he is a relatively harmless prat.'

'Yes, I'll tell Barnack's widow that next time I see her.' Micky said.

Shay nodded sadly. 'Yes, I see what you mean. He is a liability. So, what have we got to do? One, take him with us on a job. Two, find a meeting place well away from civilisation, three, dispose of the body, so it is not going to be found by anyone.'

'Exactly,' said Micky. 'Let's get down to business.'

It took them two hours to get their plans together and make a list of what they would needed. Micky went off to get some gardening tools and to buy a large-scale map from the stationers in town.

He went back to the house, and Arthur had just returned with the box he had been sent to Peterborough to collect. He made a big point of opening the box and spreading its contents over the table to impress on Arthur just how much he had trusted him to do the job. The small pile of rings, brochures, necklaces and bracelets sparkled invitingly on the old kitchen table, and Micky put his jeweller's eyepiece over his right eye and proceeded to praise the quality of the product.

He told Shay and Arthur that the goods were very valuable, but hot and they needed to be moved on at a meeting tomorrow morning. All three of them were going to go because a price had not yet been agreed and there would be some tough haggling. All three of them would be tooled up. It would be just like the old days, said Micky, and Arthur seemed to brighten up after that.

CHAPTER 11

Micky arrived at Shay and Arthurs' house at ten in the morning. It was cold and grey after yesterday's sunshine, and Micky was wearing his big sheepskin jacket. It was decided that coats all round would be the best solution, not just because it was cold, but also that the three handguns they had between them were much easier to conceal in a coat.

Shay came out to the car and asked Micky if they were leaving straight away.

'Yes, let's get this done,' was his curt reply.

'Did you get everything you wanted?'

'Yes, it's in the boot, well hidden. He won't see anything at a quick glance. It's a big boot.' Micky was driving the Jag.

Shay went back to the house and returned with Arthur, who was looking more cheerful than he did yesterday. Micky was relieved that he seemed to believe the story about the meet and possible trouble agreeing on a price. Arthur sat in the back and Shay took the front passenger seat. That is how it would have been on a normal day. Today he would have preferred to be in the back, where he could watch Arthur's every move, but it looked as though he had bought Micky's story, so this would have to do.

They drove for about half an hour along the A148 towards King's Lynn, past Fakenham, and then turned off onto a small B-road. Then they turned again onto a narrow, single lane track, with passing places every few hundred yards. The road gradually got smaller with hedges closing in on the car from either side. Grass had started to grow along a thin strip in the centre of the road.

'Do you think they will be able to find us?' Arthur said.

'Yes, I am sure they will. I haven't done business with them before, but they are not going to be idiots.' Micky said. 'They will have checked it out. Maybe even left someone here to wait for us. When we get there, don't get out of the car before you take your gun out and no silencers. There is nobody around for miles, so a shot or two won't be heard. They are too damned unwieldy when you want to get a shot off first.'

Shay heard Arthur noisily trying to get his gun out of his pocket and then unscrewing the silencer. He and Micky exchanged looks and a small shake of the head.

Micky suddenly braked and turned into a what looked like a disused farmyard. There were three large barns, close together. Two of them showed signs of a fire, and the third was left with just a skeleton of bent and twisted steel.

A burnt out tractor stood next to one of the barns. Across the other side of the yard was a row of what looked like old-fashioned pigsties. Next to these was a small brick building, possibly a workshop. Standing a little way from the yard was a derelict house, without windows, doors or a roof.

The three men got out of the car and carefully moved around the yard. Micky signalling for Shay and Arthur to check inside the two barns. Shay was quickly inside his barn because the large doors at the front had a broken section which he quickly pulled off. Arthur was having to batter his way in by kicking at a rusty hinge. Suddenly, the hinge screws gave up the fight, and the door sank to the floor.

Arthur could only have been inside the barn for half-a-minute when there was a shot and then complete silence. Micky stood, frozen to the spot. There was a sound from inside the barn; someone walking slowly. He raised his gun and pointed it towards the open barn door.

'Shay,' he called, softly at first. Then a bit louder. He was just thinking of getting into the car and driving off. Had Arthur shot Shay by mistake, thinking there was someone else in there? Christ, what would Guus say to that? Micky thought the only way out would be to shoot Arthur as well, but then he would have two bodies to get rid off.

'It's okay Micky; I got him.' Shay's voice; the words were like music to his ears. He lowered his gun and noticed how much his hand was shaking. This is too much like the old days for my liking, he thought. Maybe I ought to retire. But he knew there was no retirement in his line of business. Too many skeletons, in too many cupboards.

Shay came out of the barn looking grim. Micky knew how difficult that must have been for him. Arthur may have been an idiot and liability, but he was also Shay's mate for the last few years. Shay is a pro, but even pros have feelings.

Micky opened the boot of his car and pulled out a neatly folded body bag.

'How the hell did you get that at short notice?' Shay said.

'You know me. I've got contacts. You always need people who owe you favours, because you never know when you are going to need one.'

They walked through to the back of the barn to where Arthur's body lay on the earth floor of the barn. He was face down, and blood was spreading across the ground from a large hole in the side of his head.

They laid the body bag on the floor and lifted Arthur, Shay taking the arms and Micky the legs. They placed the body in the bag, and Shay went and fetched a shovel from the back of the car. He pointed to the area where the blood had made a dark, wet pool.

'We better take that with us,' he said, and began to skim the top of the soil off. He methodically worked until all the blood-soaked earth had been shovelled into the bag and then zipped it up.

Together they carried the body to the car. It felt a lot heavier now, and Micky wasn't looking forward to moving it to where they were going to bury it.

'Bloody hell Shay, now you have shovelled all the earth in, the bag's heavy as hell.'

'We couldn't leave all that blood lying about. We can't afford to leave a trail. That was the plan. Don't leave a single trace. Otherwise, we will be living our lives, always waiting for the knock at the door.'

Micky knew he was right, so he said nothing.

They drove back to the main road and then turned left towards Fakenham again. Then they took a right-hand turn onto the A1065 and headed for Swaffham. Micky knew a pub in Swaffham, and they stopped for some food. Neither of them wanted any food, but they both knew that the next part of the job was going to be the hardest, both physically and mentally.

Shay had nerves of steel, but he was still thinking about the frantic look on Arthur's face when he stepped out from behind that pile of old rubbish in the barn and shot his mate in the head from about ten inches. From experience, he knew these things had to be done. But it still didn't feel good.

Micky was also beginning to worry Shay. Ever since Guus came over, he had looked jumpy and nervy. Micky had lived a charmed life up until now. Almost everything he touched turned to money, and tough times always come along eventually, but if Micky was going to get through this one, he had to pull himself together.

They got back into the car and drove on to towards Thetford Forest. The plan meant finding a suitable spot in the heart of the forest, away from roads, pathways, and tracks. The problem was how heavy the bag was for two people to carry deep into the woods.

They drove around for a while, getting to know the layout and the best place to park the car without it looking suspicious. Fortunately, the day had remained as cold as it had started, and in the late afternoon, it seemed to be keeping visitors away from the forest.

They continued their drive around for another couple of miles, moving, as far as they could, deeper into the Forest. The density of the foliage made it look as though night-time had already arrived. Micky stopped the car and then began to reverse the large Jaguar into the woods. A row of bushes now shielded the car from the track, and low-hanging branches hung down only inches from the car roof.

Micky was not looking forward to this. He had grown used to telling people to do this sort of chore for him, while he sat at home waiting for the call to come through saying that the job was finished. But Guus had made it very clear that Micky needed to make sure it was done properly and that nothing could connect them to Arthur's disappearance. If Micky's plan worked as it should, no one would notice that he had gone and, if they did, he had gone to live with his brother in Australia.

It was well known in the pubs that Arthur frequented, that if you wanted an evening of solid boredom, just ask him how wonderful Australia was and what a high paying job his brother had. Without realising it, Arthur had created the perfect cover for his own disappearance.

'Come on, let's get on with this,' Micky said.

They got out of the car and were immediately shocked at the silence of a forest at dusk. Just a whisper as the light breeze ruffled the leaves at the top of the trees and the scurrying of a small animal in the bushes. Micky didn't like it at all.

They took two shovels out of the car boot and several battery lamps. They put the lamps and a hatchet into a small knapsack, and Shay slung it over his shoulder. They half lifted, half dragged the body out of the car boot and dropped it onto the soil. They then put the two shovels on top of the body bag and secured them with a couple of lengths of rope wrapped around it.

They took the handles at each end and began to carry the body slowly through the trees and deeper into the forest.

'Bloody hell,' said Micky, 'This is hard work.' His voice sounded like a shout in the silent wood. Shay wanted to tell him to keep it quiet, but Micky didn't take well to anyone telling him what to do; unless it was Guus, of course.

'Let's try dragging it,' suggested Shay. They lowered the bag until the centre of it was dragging along the forest floor. It worked well, except when the odd tree root caught the bag.

They had gone about another thirty yards or so when Micky dropped his end of the bag and stopped. 'That's far enough. My back is giving me jip,' he said.

'We haven't gone far. Not as far as we planned.'

'I know, I know, I know,' said Micky irritably. 'I didn't expect the trees and bushes to be as close together. It will be okay here.'

Shay wasn't going to argue. The sooner they started digging, the better, as far as he was concerned. Micky seemed to be wilting by the minute, and it was obvious who was going to do most of the digging. He started by carefully scraping all the leaves, twigs and other debris from an area about six feet by three. Then he picked up one of the shovels and started to dig, while Micky arranged the lamps around the rectangle where Shay had scratched the surface. The light was fading quickly now, and the lamps would soon be needed.

The first few inches were easy, although the lightness of the soil made it difficult to get a good shovel full. Micky watched Shay for a while and then joined in. It wasn't long before they hit tree roots.

'What the bloody hell can we do with these,' he said, after several hits with the sharp end of the shovel had failed to break the root.

'That's what the hatchet is for,' said Shay, picking it up and attacking the root until it broke.

'Christ, this is going to take us all night,' Micky complained.

'No, once we get through this top layer we should be okay.' Shay was more worried about the noise they were making being heard by someone taking a late-night walk along the track. When it was fully dark, they would be safer, except that then the lights might be seen. When they had to turn the lamps on, he would go and check.

They both dug some more, but the soft topsoil was still difficult to work with. When they got down beyond two feet, the going got a little easier, but Micky was still finding it hard. It was almost dark now, so he suggested that they stop and put the lamps on.

They turned two of them on, and Shay set off to circle around where they were digging to check if the lights could be seen. He quickly discovered that around fifteen yards away; nothing showed through the foliage. His problems started when he tried to circle round to get a view from every angle. He quickly realised that he couldn't tell where he was. He blundered around, fighting his way through the bushes, trying to gauge where Micky was.

He pushed another bush to one side, and an animal of some sort shot out and went past him before he could even tell what it was. It seemed to be about the size of a dog. It was obviously in full panic as it sped through the wood.

Then Shay heard a shout go up from Micky. 'What the fuck was that?'

The animal had obviously just past Micky in its mad dash to safety. At least Shay now knew where he was. He made his way back to Micky, who was standing in the partly dug grave, looking petrified.

'I had to check it out from all angles. You can't see the lights until you get close, so I think we are safe, so long as we keep the noise to a minimum. There won't be many people about now that it's nearly dark. Not unless they are up to no good, like us.'

'Or they have come for a shag on the quiet,' said Micky.

'If they do, I don't think they will be getting out of their car. It's brass monkeys unless you are digging a fucking grave.'

'Yeah, let's get on with it,' said Micky.

It took four more hours to complete the job. Digging was completed quickly, but when they came to shovel the soil back in, they discovered that they had a lot left over. Shay cursed himself for not thinking about this before. He knew he would get the blame.

'Okay,' he said quickly, 'now we just have to take shovels full of this muck and spread it around. Under bushes, around trees and anywhere else that it won't be noticed. It's late September, and the leaves are already falling. By tomorrow it will all look the same.'

Micky didn't complain, he just got on and did the job. They finished off by scraping the leaves they had moved, back onto the grave. They picked up the tools and Shay used one of the torches to find and cover over any footprints he could see. They walked slowly back to the car, stopping as they got close to make sure there was no one else around. Micky had visions of a police car just parked in front of the Jag, with a couple of coppers sitting inside, having a smoke and waiting for them to return. Fortunately, there was no one there.

They drove back, largely in silence. They were both exhausted, and their clothes and boots looked a total mess. Micky drove carefully back towards Cromer. The main roads were quiet because it was now almost midnight. When they reached Shay's house, Micky drove down the driveway at the side. Shay took the torches and the tools and put them in his shed. He told Micky that he would thoroughly wash the shovels and hatchet and then put them back in the shed. He would make sure that any soil was well dug into his garden, which was a mass of weeds and could do with digging.

Micky drove home. He went into the house and was relieved to see that Lizzie had gone to bed. He went to his bedroom and took a shower. He rolled his clothes up and put them in a bag. He would get rid of them in the morning.

Lizzie had gone to bed, but she was not asleep. She was wondering what he had been doing and why he needed a shower as soon as he came home. Surely, he hasn't started something with a girl around Cromer now. If he had, she would soon find out.

CHAPTER 12

For the past few days, Emily and Steve had been gathering information from the people who Steve had known before he left home to start his job in Norwich. They had been deliberately keeping a low profile and sticking to the story of being in Cromer for a holiday. Now, they felt that they had heard all the theories, the guesses and just a few facts about what was happening in Cromer. Had this quiet little town on the Norfolk Coast been infiltrated by a London gangster? Was there any connection between this and the murder of a local antique dealer? Why was a local police officer so certain that the murder was committed by burglars from another part of the country?

Emily and Steve sat together in their hotel bedroom and weighed up the information that they had gathered so far, and decided that it was time for them to become more proactive, but still keep a low profile.

That is why they were now sitting in a rented car on Cliff Drive, watching the big white house about fifty yards down the street. That was where Micky Naylor and his wife had lived for the past few months, and the consensus was, that if anyone matched the profile of a London gangster, it was Micky Naylor.

They had been there all day yesterday, but there had been no sign of him. Either he didn't leave the house all day, or he started very early and finished very late. Today, they had arrived much earlier, and it seemed to be paying off when, after sitting there for about thirty-five minutes, the front door opened. A man in a dark grey suit stepped outside and walked past the big Jaguar parked outside the double garage, out the large iron gates and turned right and walked down the hill. His broad shoulders and fair hair confirmed that it was Micky. He was carrying a black leather briefcase.

'Looks like a bank manager going to work,' Emily said.

'Yes, I think this means that he is going to walk to the station. It's too early for a meeting locally, and he's made a big effort to look like a successful businessman. Let's drive straight to the station.'

'Why do you think he is walking? He's got plenty of cars' Emily said.

'I don't know. Maybe he wants to be seen doing what ordinary people in the town do, or perhaps he just wants to keep fit.'

They drove past him just as he turned onto the main road. They were careful not to look at him as he strode purposefully along the pavement.

Steve said, 'We'll buy tickets and get on the train and wait to see where he sits. We need one of us in front of him and one behind. He could be going to London or maybe just to Norwich.' Steve was already turning the car into the station car park. 'I've got the camera, so I will try to get some shots of him and anyone he meets.'

'Okay, you go and get your ticket and get to the front. I'll follow when he arrives and sit behind him,' Emily said.

They had deliberately dressed as different to one another as possible. Emily was the young businesswoman off to work, with a navy suit, small briefcase and round, heavy framed glasses. With her hair scraped back and her ponytail wound into a bun, she managed to look plain, studious, and serious. Steve could hardly believe it was his pretty, fun loving Emily.

Steve had gone for a scruffy blue jeans and anorak look, with an old knapsack and the top of a flask sticking out of one side. It looked like his lunch bag, but in fact, all it held was his long lens camera, with which he was hoping to get a good shot of Micky. His hair was suitably uncombed, and his workmens boots look as though they hadn't seen polish for many months.

Emily and Steve had worked on building several different looks, so that they could carry out the necessary surveillance work, without attracting too much attention.

On the platform, there were several groups of people, who looked like regular commuters, probably to Norwich or maybe North Walsham. Emily spotted Steve walking onto the platform and making his way to the far end.

She saw Steve remove his timetable booklet from his knapsack and open it.

Five minutes later Micky arrived, carrying his briefcase. He had bought a newspaper from somewhere on his walk to the station. He moved along the platform towards where Steve was waiting. She checked her watch. The train was due in about three minutes, and a few seconds later Emily heard the familiar whistle of the train alerting passengers of its arrival.

She got out of the car and walked quickly to the ticket office, and bought her ticket. On the platform, she could see that Micky had stopped well short of Steve. There were about a dozen other people waiting for the train. It moved slowly into the station and stopped. A few people who had made the short trip from Sheringham got out, and the Cromer passengers began to join the train.

She held back until Micky had entered the carriage and took her seat a little way behind him. She could see his head and the top of the newspaper when he turned the pages. During the journey to Norwich, he did not leave his seat. As they approached Norwich station, she decided to get up and go to the door to be first out when the train stopped. She thought that is what an eager young executive would do.

She jumped off the train and moved rapidly towards the ticket barrier. Ahead of her, she saw that Steve was already through. She walked and watched where he positioned himself. He came to a stop just inside the main exit. She handed her ticket to the collector, he punched it and handed it back. She glanced to her left and saw that Micky was handing his ticket over to another collector.

From his position at the exit, Steve could see Emily walk briskly to the other exit and then pause and look around as if she was expecting someone to meet her. For a moment, he thought he had lost Naylor but then saw him disappearing into the refreshment room at the far side of the station, not far from where Emily was standing. She had also seen him and started towards the refreshment room door while watching to see if Steve agreed with her move. He nodded, and she continued inside.

Micky had gone to the counter and was waiting for a girl to fill his cup from a glass coffee pot. He turned and walked to a table, as Emily went to the other end of the counter and asked for a cup of tea. She moved to a table near the door and sat down. The room was crowded and a man, with cup in hand, asked Emily if he could share her table. It was the last thing she wanted, but it would have been rude to say no, and he might have reacted and caused a scene, so she reluctantly said yes.

'Waiting for someone?' he asked.

She ignored him, pretending she hadn't heard him.

So, he said it again.

'Oh, yes,' she said.

'Your boyfriend, is it?' he said, leaning forward with a leering grin on his face.

'No, it's my father, and he doesn't take kindly to people making a nuisance of them self,' she said sharply.

'Oh, it's like that is it,' he said, and then stood up and mumbled. 'Miss bloody lah-de-da,' and then walked away.

She looked over and saw that Micky was still sitting at his table. She could also see that he had placed the briefcase between his feet, as though there was something important inside, and he was getting reassurance from holding it with his legs.

She saw Steve come in through the door and make his way to the counter. Then she saw him notice Micky and then scan the other tables until he saw her. He got a coffee and brought it over and asked if he could share her table.

'Of course, you can,' she said.

'While it's still busy I thought we could have a chat,' Steve said.

'I just told that man over there that I am waiting for my father,' she laughed. 'Which makes you fifty-five.'

Steve turned and looked at the man. He looked uncomfortable and then got up and left.

'Obviously, he finds the stern look very off-putting, I must try it more often. So, what's the plan?' she said.

'I think he is either waiting to go down to London or waiting for someone to arrive from London, or even from somewhere else. If he is going to London, we both get tickets and go. Two of us will be better on a long journey. But if he is meeting someone, we will see what happens and take it from there; we might want to split up and take one each. We have both got plenty of cash, so we are ready for almost anything.'

'Yes, okay,' she said.

'You stay here now, looking like you are waiting for someone' he said, 'and I'll go outside and watch the incoming trains. There is a little gathering of trainspotters out there; I am going to get my camera out and mingle with them.'

As Steve stepped out of the café, they were announcing the arrival of the London train. The station suddenly came alive with porters pushing a variety of trolleys down the platform towards the train as it made its way slowly over the final few yards to stop just short of the buffers in Norwich Station. Two men in uniforms were pushing a large cage packed with Royal Mailbags.

The train stopped and immediately the carriage doors were flung open. People poured from the train and hurried towards the exit. Steve had positioned himself a short way from the ticket collectors. Three ragged queues formed quickly, and he was able to pay attention to every arriving passenger.

Steve's attention was attracted to a smallish man, wearing an ill-fitting, brown, double-breasted suit, and a wide-brimmed trilby. Apart from the outfit looking very London East End, he was carrying a briefcase that was the same as the one Micky had. Steve thought it a coincidence, but as it was a style that he had seen many times before, and must be available in hundreds of shops up and down the country, it was only a minor coincidence.

The man walked with a confident swagger, his wide-legged trousers flapping as he went. Through the ticket barrier, he turned left, just as Steve hoped he would. Was this the first insight as to how this operation worked? Could they get a start today on gathering some evidence as to what was happening?

He was heading for the station café, and Steve knew that Emily would spot the man immediately. He walked through the café door, and Emily had to have a second glance to confirm that the little man in the brown suit was there and not a figment of her imagination. She had to force herself to look away. It was as if he had just stepped out of an American gangster film. She felt sure that nobody would have given him a second glance in London, but in Norfolk, it was a little unusual.

However, when Naylor greeted him with a warm handshake, he didn't look in any way surprised. The man sat at the table and then Emily noticed the matching briefcases. If they changed them there, at the table, she would have a perfect view. But after a few moments conversation, they both stood up and made for the door.

They came out of the café and walked straight into the Gents toilets next door. They were in and out in seconds, and Emily guessed that the switch had been made. That did not matter. Now, Steve would be trying to get pictures of how the operation was organised and how far it spread. Some of the gossip in the town was that it even reached mainland Europe, so this was just a start.

She looked around for Steve and saw him in a small crowd of kids and older men, some with notebooks, some with cameras and almost all of them with little bags on their backs. Taking your lunch and tea around with you meant not having to miss even one train number. Steve moulded in with the trainspotters far too easily, she thought.

The man in the brown suit and Naylor shook hands again, and Micky turned and walked towards a platform, on the opposite side of the station. There was no train at that platform yet, but Micky sat down to wait on a bench, keeping his briefcase close to him.

The man in the brown suit, checked his watch and then walked to the ticket barrier and spoke to a man in a British Railways uniform.

The cleaners were beginning to leave the London train, and the ticket collector waved the brown suit man through. He walked towards the front of the train and boarded it close to where the trainspotters were assembled. Emily hoped that Steve had managed to get a shot of the man in the brown trilby.

Ten minutes later the London train began to move out, just as the Sheringham and Cromer train was arriving. Emily could see Steve, ready with his camera, and as soon as the rear coach of the London train went past, he began to shoot across the lines at what appeared to be the arriving local train. But Emily was certain that Steve's lens was firmly fixed on Micky. It was touch and go, but even from that distance, she could tell by Steve's body language, that he had the shot they wanted.

He came walking back towards her along the platform. Emily turned and walked out of the station and stood with her back to the wall, looking at the row of taxis. Steve came out the station, looked around and saw her standing there. He came over towards her, and she could see that he was trying not to smile.

'I take it that you got the shot?' she said.

'Two or three of both of them I hope.'

She was fighting to keep her serious persona but could not stop herself and flung her arms around him. She realised that hugging was not very professional when you were on surveillance duty, but no one was looking.

Steve laughed. 'That was like getting a hug from a schoolmistress.'

'This look is beginning to age me,' Emily said. 'What are we going to do next?'

'Get on the local train and stay as far away as we can from 'our man'. Then just follow him back home, to make sure he doesn't meet any other business partners on the way.'

Emily went ahead and got into the first carriage. There were only a few people travelling, and she had a selection of seats from which to choose. She settled for one right at the back, so that she could be off first and through the barriers quickly.

Steve spotted Micky in the front carriage, sitting against the window. Steve wanted to be behind him but didn't want to turn back once Micky had seen him. He took his camera out and made a show of photographing the engine, as it stood hissing and wheezing at the end of the platform. Then he put his camera away and walked back beside the train and chose the middle carriage.

When they arrived at Cromer, Steve got onto the platform and saw that Emily was already through the barriers and no doubt going to wait somewhere close by until Micky passed her. At a very safe distance, she would then drop in behind him and follow.

When Micky was walking down the main shopping street in the town, Steve would go past her and tail him home. When Emily got to where the impressive Church towered over the town, she stopped to look in a shop window, and Steve moved quickly to take her place. When Steve turned into Cliff Drive, Micky was already rounding the curve that leads to the steep hill and grand clifftop houses. Steve didn't go past the curve in the road. He could see Micky's house from there and watched him walk into the front garden.

CHAPTER 13

Micky returned to the house and found that Lizzie wasn't there. He was slightly irritated that she was out again, but on the other hand, he could spend some time looking at the stuff Reg Nixon had brought for him from London. He missed working with Reg. He was a funny little bugger, with his oversized, padded-shoulder suits and American gangster hats, but underneath all that show, he was a real pro.

He had been Micky's right-hand man when they operated from London, and with all this crap that he had to deal with, he wished Reg was around to sort things out. He was a good ten years older than Micky and had a knowledge of London's underworld that was second to none. Everybody in the business seemed to know him, and almost all of them respected Reg. He was a feisty little sod and scared the hell out of many people, but he was a man of his word and totally reliable. He never seemed to get flustered and generally could find a solution to most problems.

The trouble was that when things started to get too hot for Micky in London, the only person that he could trust to run the acquisition side of the business, was Reg. He knew how to keep people in line, particularly if they were getting greedy. He had a good understanding of the business and what sold well and what didn't. He was also pretty good at estimating the value of items and understood that when you've nicked something in the middle of the night and you don't know if the householder might come back at any moment, that there is bound to be some junk amongst the good stuff. Even millionaires can get sentimental over certain items, but you don't have time to pick and choose.

Micky sat in his study overlooking the North Sea and realised that he was tired. Yesterday had been one of the toughest days he could remember, and he had had some tough days, particularly when it was all turning to shit in Berlin. But yesterday was one day he wouldn't forget. In his time, he had had to get rid of quite a few people, but that was for a good reason. They had been stealing from him or skimming off the profits, blackmailing or threatening to grass on him. These were all good reasons, but to have to kill poor old Arthur, just because he had done something stupid, seemed harsh to Naylor.

And then there was the bloody pantomime of burying him. Without Shay, he just couldn't have got the job done. He intended to give him a good bonus for that, and it must have been tough for him because Arthur was his mate. He would also let Guus know that they had done what he asked them to do and with a bit of luck he would leave them alone to get on with business. Then he thought that if there is someone feeding information back to Guus, he probably already knows.

Micky went over to his drinks cupboard and got a nice bottle of malt whisky out. He poured himself a good measure and sat down at his desk again. He emptied the contents of the briefcase Reg had brought to him and started sifting through the pile of necklaces, bracelets, rings, earrings, brooches, watches, and small ornaments. Micky's experienced eye was seeing the value of the jewellery in hard currency. Later, when he felt less tired, he would methodically go through it all, assessing its likely value, and what he might get for it on the black market; what he and Guus liked to call 'the hot market'. He also roughly divided it up between what he thought they could get away with selling here, in the UK, and what would be safest to send over to mainland Europe. Micky was a safety-first man, so around 70 percent of the items would go to Europe.

He heard the front door open and then close again. That was Lizzie coming in. It was 11.30. Where could you go in Cromer until this hour? It was time he had a word with her.

He quickly put the jewellery in his office safe and opened his study door. Lizzie was just beginning to climb the stairs.

'Where have you been?' he snapped at her.

'Where have you been Micky,' she replied in that infuriatingly calm way she had. 'You tell me where you have been and I will tell you where I have been?' She flicked her long black hair over her shoulder and smiled at him.

'I've been working. That's what I've been doing. Earning us some money.'

'And what about yesterday,' she added. 'Out all day and coming home late looking as though you had been rolling about in the mud. I saw you come in at almost midnight. I looked out of my bedroom window. The security light went on, and you looked a mess.'

'The car broke down, and I had to get underneath it to fix the problem,' he said, but even he didn't think it sounded very convincing.

Lizzie said, 'I went to see a friend; she has boyfriend problems,' She didn't care whether he believed her or not.

'What friend? You don't have any friends here. What's her name.' he said sharply, a little concerned that she might be making friends.

She was getting fed up with the conversation. 'I'm not telling you her name. I don't want you going around to see her. You would finish up fucking her, just like you did to my old friends in London.'

She turned and walked up the stairs. Micky didn't say any more; he was trying to think who had told her that. It wouldn't be Janis or Judy; they loved it. It must have been that bitch, Vickie. The trouble was, despite all that had happened between them, he still wanted Lizzie. She was infuriating, stubborn and always had the last word. But she is still a real looker, and he still fancied her.

Lizzie was a tall, slim young woman in her mid-twenties. She was one of those people that managed to look elegant, whatever she was doing. She was well educated and intelligent. In fact, although Micky had always let her know who was the boss in their relationship, he always felt a little bit intimidated by her. She had an air of mystery about her, which is what attracted him to her in the first place.

There were many girls of her sort drifting around London at that time. Girls from good families who loved the hippy stuff that was coming out of the USA. Smoking pot, love not war, flowers in their hair and all that sort of nonsense that Micky despised.

What the changing times did was give a chance of success to up and coming working-class lads like him, who had been clever enough to make a quid or two. They could now get girls like Lizzie. A few years ago it would have been out of the question, but now the rough and ready boys were in demand from this sort of girl. A few years before, they were looking for posh young toffs, who knew which knife and fork to use and didn't have to bother about earning a living because Daddy could always get them a job.

So, Micky thought, why worry too much about Lizzie, there were plenty of girls like her just ready and waiting for him.

He woke early the next morning, with the happenings of recent days running wild in his mind. Suddenly the cosy quietness of Cromer was beginning to feel more like a trap that he had built for himself and then walked straight into. There were too many distractions and he really ought to be concentrating on running the business.

He got himself a coffee and sat at the kitchen table. At least Lizzie wouldn't get up until he had gone out. He had no meetings arranged for the day, but he thought he would go and see Shay and they could talk through what needed to be done next. Shay was a very cool character and would talk common sense.

The phone rang, and to Micky's surprise, it was Brian Brooks, the Sergeant at the local police station. It was an unwritten rule that he would not make calls to Micky.

'Is that Micky,' he asked, tentatively.

'Yes Brian, what's the problem?'

'We need to meet. I've got some info you need to have' he said.

'When and where,' Micky wanted to keep the conversation on the phone to a minimum.

'Salthouse. Park near the pond. Walk to the beach. Two-thirty this afternoon. Okay with you?'

'Okay,' said Micky and the phone went dead. He wanted to ask why, but he knew that Brooks wouldn't be calling him unnecessarily. Not something else to worry about, he thought.

He finished his coffee, grabbed his green wax jacket, wellington boots and went out to his car. He left his Jaguar and took his old Land Rover, which was parked alongside the garage. As he left, he thought he saw Lizzie watching from her bedroom window.

He drove to Shay's house and found him digging his previously untouched garden. This was why Shay was so good. He was establishing a reason for buying the shovels and a hatchet.

'How's it going Shay?' he asked.

'Good. I'm quite enjoying this. I might take up gardening. It keeps you fit,' he replied.

'I got a call from Brooks this morning. He wants a meet.'

'Did he say why?' Shay asked.

'No, he called from a box. He knows not to say too much on the phone. Wants me to meet him at Salthouse this afternoon, well away from anyone who might know us.'

'Want me to come along?' Shay asked.

'Better not, we don't want to spook him. I don't think he'll cause any problems; he has got as much to lose as us.

'I tell you what, I'll give you a hand with the digging,' said Micky, taking his jacket off.

Shay looked at him in surprise. 'What?'

'Didn't think this was your scene. It's bloody hard work.'

Micky picked up the shovel and began to dig. He lasted about twenty minutes and then said, 'I think this is doing my back in.' and put the shovel down. 'I'll call in on the way back and tell you what Brooks wanted.'

'Okay,' said Shay with a smile.

Micky Naylor arrived at the pond at Salthouse at a quarter-past-two. There were several cars parked there, but he didn't know what Brian Brooks drove, so he couldn't tell if he had already arrived. Salthouse and the neighbouring village of Cley-next-the-sea, are symbolic of much of the North Norfolk coast.

Their beauty is in the bleakness of the marshes, and the villages of flintstone cottages, that seem to have been placed haphazardly in little groups along narrow lanes that twist and turn and go nowhere. It was a lovely day, with a magnificent sky that can change dramatically in seconds and reflect its beauty in the streams and pools that intersect the fields of grass and rushes.

Naylor was oblivious of all this around him as he got out of the Land Rover, put on his jacket and boots and set off towards the sea. It was cold, but the pale blue sky, tinged with thin white cloud managed to inject a little heat into the landscape when the watery sun shone through. There was very little wind, and even Micky Naylor found himself enjoying the isolation that the flat marshes created. He could see a few figures here and there on the horizon, but otherwise, there was no sign of human life. There were plenty of birds flying around, but Micky just did not get why anyone would want to look at them. Birds do what birds do, and it was of no interest to him.

He was, however, keeping a close lookout for Sergeant Brooks, but he didn't see any sign of him until he reached the beach. He stopped, looked around, and there he was coming up behind him.

'Hello Brian,' Micky said as he shook Brooks' hand. 'How are you?'

'I'm okay thanks, but I thought I'd better let you know that there are two journalists in town, wanting to know how we are getting on with the Morris Barnack investigation.'

'What did you tell them?' Micky asked, alarmed by this new development.

'I said we were certain it was just a burglary gone wrong. An out of town gang that just came here for some easy pickings.'

'And what did they say?' asked Micky.

'Not a lot, but I think they believed what I told them.'

The two men began to walk slowly along the path on top of the low embankment that divided the beach from the marshland behind.

'And when was this?'

Brooks thought for a moment and then said, 'About three or four days ago. I didn't tell you before because I needed to find out who they were and who they were working for.'

Micky nodded his understanding. 'And now you know?'

'Yes, they're a young couple, mid-twenties. Very well thought of. They came to the fore when they solved a triple murder in the fens near Peterborough. From what I have been able to find out, they caught the interest of the media at first because they are young and good-looking, and that seems to be enough to make you a celebrity these days. But they have gone on to several other successful investigations and proved it wasn't just a flash in the pan.'

'And you think it was the same two that came to see you?'

'I know it was. I've seen pictures of them. I got them sent to me.'

'So, what are we going to do about them?' asked Micky.

'There is nothing I can do,' said Brooks. 'I was sailing close to the wind after Barnack's demise. That only came just in time for me.'

'What do you mean?' asked Micky.

Brooks looked at Micky in surprise. 'Barnack was telling everyone he was going to write to the Chief Constable and ask for a meeting. He was going to accuse me of turning a blind eye to your activities. I thought that's why you topped him?'

Micky stopped and stared at Brooks, his face drained of colour. 'No, that was a fucking accident. I sent them round to rough him up a bit to stop him mouthing off about me. He came in with a baseball bat and caught one of my blokes with a couple of headshots. The guy went berserk and stabbed Barnack. I knew nothing of him trying to get the Chief Constable involved.

'Well, lucky for me,' said Brooks, as cool as anything. 'I was getting ready to do a runner.'

Micky decided not to tell Brooks what had happened to Arthur. There might come a time when Brooks was surplus to requirements, and he didn't want him to be nervous at a time like this.

'So, what happens now?' Micky asked.

'Steady as you go. I'll keep doing a little bit here and there about Barnack, but it won't lead anywhere. It is this other pair who are more worrying. They are smart and pushy, like most journalists, but if anything happened to them, the media would be all over us. They are the golden couple at the minute, so we have got to be careful. I'm going to have to keep right out of their way. You can perhaps put a few feelers out to find where they are staying and what they are doing. It might be a good idea to suspend activities for a while.'

'Yes, you could be right,' Micky said as they turned to make their way back to the cars.

Underneath, Micky was furious. He had invested big money into getting Brooks on his side, and now he was going to walk away. He was on the brink of exploding and telling Brooks how this was still his responsibility. Or asking for his money back. But he obviously had written this off, and there was nothing Micky could do now. Guus would go bloody crazy if Micky decided to top the local copper. But he would get his own back, one day. He would have the pleasure of burying the fucking idiot in Thetford Forest. And he would do it on his own if necessary, but now was not the time. Things would settle down, and scores could be settled later.

Brooks said that he would stay at the beach for a while, to let Micky get clear. Micky couldn't even be bothered to shake his hand. He waved a hand in the air and quickened his pace. When he reached the road, he turned and looked back, but Brooks was nowhere to be seen.

Micky took his boots and jacket off and threw them into the back of the Land Rover with such force that a young family feeding the ducks close by all turned to look at him. Micky grinned sheepishly at them, climbed into the driver's seat and turned the Land Rover around and headed for Shay's house.

If he had driven just a few hundred yards down the road, before turning around, he would have seen Lizzie's little Ford car parked outside her cottage retreat. He might have thought that was where her friend lived, but they both knew that her friend didn't exist. And Lizzie had passed the pond only ten minutes before and failed to see Micky's Land Rover parked at the side of the road. Because, just as Micky was distracted by his problems, Lizzie was distracted by Will. Although it was only five minutes earlier that they walked into the house, they were already in bed.

CHAPTER 14

It was the third day that Emily and Steve had spent following Micky and each time they found out a little more about how he ran the operation and who he was dealing with. The photos that Steve got at Norwich railway station, he had sent to Martin Yates, who was going to show them to his informants in London to get the identities checked.

Yesterday was almost a waste of time, but it was salvaged in the end. Still using the hire car, they had followed Micky to a house on the outskirts of Cromer, at the back of the town. They parked some way down the road, and because there seemed to be nothing happening at the front of the house, Steve walked through two fields to the rear. He came back after about half an hour to report that Micky seemed to be digging the garden with another man. He thought that the other man fitted the description that Eric had given them for one of Micky's heavies, whose name was Shay.

'Are you sure they were digging the garden?' Emily asked. 'Could they have been burying something?'

'No, just digging. Quite leisurely,' Steve said. 'Not the usual activity for a master criminal.'

They stayed where they were for a while, and after about an hour, Micky came out and got into the Land Rover. Steve followed at a good distance behind. The Land Rover was comparatively easy to tail. It was distinctive, high-roofed and slow. It meant that Steve could happily be two cars behind and still see the Land Rover.

He saw it slow as Micky moved to the left and parked it on the side of the road. Steve had reacted quickly, and they were safely parked behind a small row of cars outside a builders' merchants. Emily, from the passenger seat, saw Micky go into a telephone kiosk on the street corner. He was there for some time, and a little queue gathered around the kiosk. He eventually came out and went into a pub on the other side of the road.

Surveillance is no fun, thought Emily. You sit and look at the street, with ordinary people doing ordinary things. You dare hardly look at each other, in case something dramatic happens and you miss it. And you wait and concentrate for the moment when your target comes out of the pub, gets in his Land Rover and drives off. That sounds fine if it wasn't for the fact that you had just sat and looked at a pub door for an hour and a half.

They followed him down to the front, and he turned left onto Runton Road. Steve slowed, almost as if he was going to stop, and let two cars pass him. He then speeded up again and maintained a steady distance between them and Micky. People all naturally look at the car behind them, and sometimes, the car behind will do something that attracts your attention. But three cars behind and you would have to do something quite dramatic to get noticed.

The road which runs East along the North Norfolk coast, was hilly, winding and narrow, and particularly difficult when passing traffic in one of the many pretty villages. Steve knew that following as far behind as he was, he might get held up at any time. But he also knew that he could quickly catch up.

They got held up at the crossroads in Sheringham but had caught up by the time they reached Welbourne and then on to Salthouse. There was a lovely pond there that attracted different birds. It was one of his favourite places as a little boy. To his surprise, Micky stopped just before he reached the pond and pulled onto the grass verge.

Steve drove passed and stopped a little way down the road. I think we could risk getting out and getting a closer look at Micky, Steve said. I want to know what he is up to. This is not his sort of habitat at all.

As it happens, Steve and Emily had discussed last night changing her appearance. She thought that Micky had given her a second look when she walked in the station café. It was no more than a glance that most attractive girls of her age would get from a man. But if Micky was good at remembering faces, he might get suspicious. That is why Emily visited the chemist and bought some blonde hair dye. She spent an hour, with Steve's help, applying the dye and washing it off in the bathroom that adjoined their bedroom. So yesterday she had light brown hair, tied back in a ponytail, today she was blonde, with soft curls, which were just longer than shoulder length.

'Let's walk close together, like soppy young lovers,' Emily said. 'It's a good disguise.'

'What sort of disguise is that?' said Steve, 'we are soppy young lovers.'

They got out of the car and walked, with their arms around each other. There were several people, including one or two children, looking at the ducks and swans. Steve saw Naylor walking across the road. He was wearing a heavy waxed jacket and wellington boots. He didn't even glance their way; his attention was on the small pathway the led down to the beach.

They watched him walk off into the distance and then went back to the car and sat inside. Micky had merged into the flat landscape of the marshes. It was possible to see as far as the raised bank that divided the beach from the wetlands behind. They could see a few miniature figures walking along the bank, but they were so small that once you looked away, it was difficult to find them again. Emily took some binoculars off the shelf under the car dashboard. She would wind the window down and look towards the distant bank.

'It's too far. You just can't see enough detail.' She offered the binoculars to Steve, but he shook his head.

'No, you're right, they won't help us. I could walk out there and see what is going on. Whatever it is, he wants to be to be well away from spying eyes. But I think if I did go out there looking for him it could completely blow our cover.'

'Yes, let's just sit here and wait till he comes back. Then we can decide what to do.'

They didn't have long to wait. In a little less than an hour, the now familiar figure of Micky came walking back. He was around six feet tall and quite a stocky build. He didn't look particularly fit and seemed to be carrying some excess weight, but he looked as though he could handle himself in a fight. His fair, almost blonde unruly mop of hair made him easy to spot.

He walked across the road, took his boots and coat off and flung them so hard into the back of the Land Rover that a family feeding the ducks stopped and looked across at him. He climbed into the driver's seat.

'Who's in a paddy then?' said Emily.

'Yes, he didn't seem happy at all. Well, let's hope it's nothing trivial,' said Steve.

'Are we going to follow him?' Emily asked.

'I don't know. I think I'd like to see if anyone else that we know comes walking back from the beach.'

Micky turned the Land Rover around and headed back towards Cromer

Emily nodded. 'Yes, that would be interesting. Who wouldn't want to be seen with him?'

'About half the population of Cromer,' laughed Steve. 'I don't think he is going win any popularity polls.'

The answer to Emily's question came about fifteen minutes later when a lone man came walking back along the beach path.

'I recognise him,' said Steve, quickly trying to think where he had seen him.

'Sergeant Brian Brooks,' said Emily, 'expert in homemade crime statistics.'

'Well, that explains a lot,' said Steve. 'Christ, I think he's coming this way.'

Brooks had turned left and was walking past the pond towards where Steve had parked. Emily was getting ready to slide into the seat well, but Steve had nowhere to go. Fortunately, Brooks was distracted by a bus that was passing at that moment, and he turned away from them to avoid the bus. He then opened the door of the car in front, and without giving them a glance, jumped into the driver's seat and drove away.

CHAPTER 15

Steve and Emily drove back to Cromer and went back to their hotel to talk things over. They had made very good progress in the last few days, but their information was still very sketchy, and a lot of it was guesswork.

'Let's ask Eric to meet us, and we can see if he has anything to tell us,' Steve said. 'It might help to confirm some of the things that are still not clear.'

Steve called him, and they agreed to meet at a pub in a small village a few miles out of town. The bar of the pub was full of locals, so they moved to the lounge at the back. It was a smallish room and had obviously been part of the landlord's living area. Now it was more of a snug than a lounge, but as they were the only ones in there, it suited them very well.

They quickly told Eric of their meeting with Sergeant Brooks at the police station, Micky's trip to Norwich and then his meeting with Brooks at Salthouse.

'How have you got on?' Steve said. 'What is the gossip around the town.'

'Well, cutting through some of the more ridiculous flights of fantasy, most sensible people seem to think that Micky Naylor is most probably a crook and it seems likely that he is the man that you are looking for. But, apart from moving into the town at approximately the time your man was supposed to have left London, I haven't heard any reasons to support that.'

Eric explained that Morris Barnack was the sort of person you find in every town; always wanting to be opposite to everyone else. To most people, he was a know-all and a general pain in the arse. When someone told him, that Naylor dealt in jewellery and had just bought a big house on Cliff Drive, complete with swimming pool, Barnack immediately labelled him a thief and a gangster. He was ready to tell anyone who would listen, and a good many who couldn't get away from him, just what he thought about Naylor and his so-called business.

Things were made worse when two human gorillas moved to the town and turned out to be working for Naylor. For Barnack, that was all the proof he needed and doubled his efforts at getting the town to turn on Naylor.

Unfortunately for him, most people were fed up with his ranting about this and that. Yellow parking lines outside his shop or the council spending too much on improving the Promenade and Pier. And then the refuse collections were on the wrong day and at the wrong time; too many fish and chip shops spoiling the nature of the town; the list was endless.

Much as they were suspicious of Naylor and his men, most people could not bring themselves to support Barnack. Then when he was murdered, everyone felt very bad about not agreeing with him.

'So, did the mood in the town change?' asked Emily.

'It is very strange now, and I think people are nervous. They're almost certain that Naylor is bad news, but that is just whispered when people meet in private. They are scared because of what happened to Barnack; they are confused as to why the investigation into his murder seems to be going nowhere. Some feel that they might have got it all wrong and that Naylor is a genuine businessman. And, I was told this afternoon that one of the two heavies seem to have left town, so maybe Naylor has realised that he needs to change the way he runs things.'

'Do you think he has really left town?' Emily asked.

Eric shrugged. 'Who knows. He could have gone on holiday, or have gone back to London for some reason. They used to be inseparable apparently, and now one drinks alone. And he doesn't talk to anyone, except to order his beer. Any efforts to include him in the banter at the bar is met with an icy stare, so people stay away from him.'

'This is all good information Eric,' said Steve 'and we do appreciate what you are doing for us. And remember we don't want you doing anything that might put you in danger. These little bits of chatter are all we expected from you. Just keep doing the same, and we will be very grateful.'

'It's no problem,' said Eric. 'I feel as though I am doing something to help the old hometown fight off some nasty intruders. I'm ready to see this one through.'

They thanked Eric, and he stood up to leave, because his girlfriend and bookkeeper, Susan would have his dinner on the table in twenty minutes. Then he stopped and turned back to Emily and Steve.

'There is one other thing that you might try,' he said. 'Naylor's wife is a real looker and gets around the town a bit, doing shopping here and there, and to everyone's surprise, she seems okay. Polite, friendly, and quiet. Won't be drawn into any conversation, except the weather and things like that.'

'Do you remember Will Bliss from school?' he asked Steve.

'Super Stud,' Steve laughed. 'How could anyone forget Will?'

'Yes,' said Eric, 'Well, I happen to know, because Will told me that he's having an affair with this fabulous looking girl. It was when the Naylors must have only just arrived, and he obviously didn't realise that this was a dangerous game he was playing. Lizzie, that's her name, told Will straight away that she was married to Naylor and that he treated her badly and was no good. But you know what Will is like, happy go lucky, head in the clouds. Even though she warned him, he was so smitten with her that he didn't grasp just how dangerous her husband might be.

'Even now she and Naylor are seldom seen together, and Will is increasingly seen with her. I think that Will might be able to help you with some information, and you can warn him about Naylor and tell him he is playing with fire.'

'Yes,' said Steve, 'that would be excellent to find someone close to them. And I would like to meet up with Will again. He is a real character, but at school, we never believed his sexual prowess was as good as the stories he told. From what you say, Super Stud is for real.'

'Oh, yes,' laughed Eric, 'Will is for real all right. The trouble is the blokes on the crab boats reckon that there is a lot of young women holidaymakers who are missing Will and may not come back next year. They say the local tourist office is very worried.'

'I think I would like to meet Will,' Emily said, with a smile.

'There is no chance of that. I'm not letting you near him,' Steve laughed.

'We have one more day of following Naylor around, and then I will go and have a chat with Will. If you happen to see him tomorrow could you tell him that I am around and would like to catch up with him on Friday? Don't tell him what it's about. Say I'm catching up with the old crowd.'

'Okay, I'll do that, got to rush now,' and with that, he went.

Emily looked at Steve and smiled, 'I think you'd better tell me all about Super Stud.'

CHAPTER 16

The art of surveillance requires patience, concentration, and luck in equal measures. That was the conclusions reached by Emily and Steve as they started their fourth day of following Micky Naylor to try and understand the way his criminal organisation functioned.

They both believed that what he was doing was criminal and it almost most certainly involved the theft and resale of expensive jewellery.

The operation seemed to involve a series of couriers, no doubt moving the stolen goods and money. Since moving away from London, these courier routes must have lengthened and consequently made them more difficult to manage. Equally, hiding the hub of criminal activity was far more difficult in a place like Cromer than it had been in London.

Micky Naylor had flaunted his wealth in London and eventually been driven out by the police. He came to Cromer, bought himself a police officer and thought he could go back to his old lifestyle. In London, if anyone stepped out of line, his heavies would soon sort the problem with a few threats and some strong-arm stuff to prove the point.

In Cromer, unless you worked very hard at being anonymous, peoples' lives were there for everyone to see. And they were not prepared to live in fear in the shadows. There would always be someone who would speak up, even if their opinions were based on unjustified guesswork. But Emily and Steve were now certain that suspicion of wrongdoing directed at Micky Naylor was justified, and they were determined to get to the truth.

As this was the fourth day, they changed their routine. They had parked at the bottom of the hill on Cliff Drive, round the bend where the road meets Church Street. They had been there since seven in the morning, and now cars were arriving to park within easy reach of the beach or shops.

The experience of the last three days had shown that when Naylor left his house at the top of the hill, he always came this way, whether on foot or in one of his cars. Today was no exception, and at nine-thirty his large black Jaguar came rolling around the corner and stopped at the main the road. Steve waited until he pulled away towards the town centre and then followed.

At a comfortable distance behind, Steve followed the big Jag in his little rented blue Ford Prefect. They went through the Runtons, both busy villages with large caravan sites, which turned them into bustling small towns during the holiday season.

Overnight there had been heavy rainfall, but it had moved on into the North Sea now, leaving a few angry black clouds in an otherwise bright blue sky. The strong breeze kept the temperature down, and the blue sea was full of small white-topped waves, racing towards the beaches.

When they reached Sheringham, Micky Naylor turned right to go into the town, but as soon as he crossed the railway line, he drove into the municipal car park and parked near the exit. Steve followed into the car park, but carried on to the next pay and display ticket machine. As he got out to buy the ticket, Steve noticed that Micky Naylor was getting his from the machine near the exit. The good law-abiding citizen that he was.

Emily jumped out of the car and was ready to move if Micky left the car park quickly. Steve parked the little Ford and was glad to see other cars now coming in. The rain had stopping and the sun coming out would quickly bring the people into town, and they needed plenty of people to hide them while they followed Micky.

Steve and Emily had adopted a student look today. They both wore the anoraks they kept for riding on the Lambretta, even though they didn't use it much these days. Steve said it kept him in touch with his younger days, Emily said he was saving it for a mid-life crisis. With knapsacks on their backs, they looked like a couple of students. Emily kept her hood up, partly because of the cold wind and partly because she hated her blond hair. When they first had the idea, as a way of making her look different, she couldn't wait to put the hair colouring on and see what she looked like.

When she first looked at the results in the mirror, she thought it looked okay. A bit washed out because of her pale complexion perhaps, but all right. The blonde seemed to drain all colour from her face. It made her look weak and ill. By last night she had grown to hate her hair. She wanted to be herself again, with her light brown hair and her ponytail. Steve said it had served its purpose, so tomorrow she could go to the hairdressers and become a light brunette again. But for now, her anorak hood was providing her disguise.

They pretended to be looking for something in the boot of the car until they saw Naylor head towards the exit. They waited until he turned left towards the main street leading down to the beach. Then they walked quickly to the exit, just in time to see Naylor walking quite slowly towards the seafront. Inevitably, he was carrying a briefcase, which looked very similar to the one he had at Norwich station.

Emily crossed the road as if she intended to go into a shop on the other side. She moved up a little closer to Naylor as he walked down the opposite pavement to her. Steve kept his position. They were just playing safe and making sure that they did not lose sight of him. Steve's view was suddenly blocked by a small group of pedestrians gathered around, looking at something one of them had just purchased. He saw Emily stop and look in a shop window. That was their signal that Naylor had gone into somewhere. When Steve reached that point, the only place he could have gone was into a bank. He looked across at Emily. She nodded and turned back to the shop window. Steve wandered on down the street.

It was almost an hour when Naylor came out of the Bank, checked his watch, and walked leisurely down the street towards the front. Emily had moved along on the opposite side of the road, almost keeping level with him, but appearing to show more interest in the shop windows than watching Naylor. But Steve knew she wouldn't miss anything and any move that Naylor made she would signal to him.

Then Naylor turned left and disappeared. Emily had also stopped and was looking in a shop window. Steve walked on to where Emily was standing on the other side of the road. Naylor had gone into a pub.

Steve walked across the road, calling out a greeting to Emily as if they were friends meeting unexpectedly.

'I'm going to go in and see if he has met someone in there,' he said. 'There is a little café just back there. See if you can get a seat near the window. He may be meeting more than one. We might have to split up and follow.'

Emily nodded and then said. 'There are three men about to go into the pub. If you tag onto to them, it will look as though you are all together.'

Steve gave her a quick embrace and then walked across the road, and went into the pub, keeping close to the three men. There were already six or seven men, all with drinks in hand, standing near the bar. Naylor sat on his own at a table near the back wall of the bar. His briefcase was on the seat next to him.

He was dressed like a businessman in dark grey suit, but he didn't stand out amongst the other men in their working clothes. It was one of those pubs that was just smart enough for white collar workers, but not too polished to keep the blue-collar drinkers away. Even Steve in his anorak, which immediately marked him as young and trendy, felt very comfortable. He ordered a pint from the woman behind the bar. She looked a woman in her sixties. Her face was very pale and wrinkled, but she had made a valiant attempt to paper over the cracks. Her lipstick was bright red and plentiful and not always where her lips were. The eye makeup was fierce, giving her a quite witch-like appearance.

But her customers obviously loved her. She laughed and joked with them and called everyone 'my darling', including Steve, who she seemed particularly pleased to meet. She asked him if he was on holiday, which he said he was, and then suddenly realised that she was doing a good job at building his cover. She asked him if he was staying here, in Sheringham, which he thought it best to say he was.

'Who are you here with?' she asked.

'My girlfriend,' he said, beginning to feel a little embarrassed.

'Have you come out for a rest my darling,' she said, to the amusement of the men at the bar.

'Leave him alone Gwen; you'll get the town a bad name,' one of the men said. He turned to Steve and said with a grin, 'sorry about that mate, we're still waiting for Gwen to grow up, but I don't think it will happen now.'

'You know you love me just the way I am,' she said, giggling like a teenager.

Gwen had done a great job at getting Steve established in the pub, and although he had just planned to stay a short time, he now felt that he could remain as long as necessary.

The door opened, and a tall, well-dressed man came in. The man looked in his fifties, with greying hair. He was immaculately turned out in a pinstriped dark blue suit, highly polished shoes and he was carrying a briefcase, exactly like Naylor's.

Gwen immediately greeted him in a tone of voice completely different from the way she spoke to her other customers.

'Good morning Mr Harris; your friend is over there. Your usual to drink?' The whole room had gone quiet for Gwen's performance, of what she obviously considered to be a posh voice. One of the other men in the pub tried to stifle a giggle, and she glared at him. She filled a glass with whatever Mr Harris's favourite beer was.

She took the drink to their table, with another one for Naylor. 'You can move into the dining room whenever you want my darling' she said. 'It's closed today, but I've laid the table for you, and the chef has come in to cook for you.'

'Thank you very much,' said Harris. Steve thought he detected a slight foreign accent.

The two men stood up immediately and went into the dining room, each carrying a briefcase. Steve thought that they might have already done the swap. There was no way he could know. There was nothing more to do here in the bar, so Steve finished his beer and put his glass on the bar top. Fortunately, Gwen was deep in conversation with one of the men at the other end of the bar, so Steve slipped out without anyone noticing.

He walked across the road to the small café. He saw Emily sitting at a table in the window. There were only about eight tables in the small café, and only three were being used. Emily had a good view of the pub entrance, although it was partially hidden by the net curtain that hung across the lower half of the window. By sitting up straight and stretching upwards, she could see the door. If she ducked her head down a little, she could see quite well through the net curtain. Steve sat down opposite her on a chair that was partially hidden by the window frame.

'Did you see the other one arrive?' Steve asked.

'Yes, the same sort of briefcase,' Emily replied. 'Any idea who it was?'

'The woman behind the bar called him Mr Harris, and he only said a few words, but I thought there was a slight accent. I couldn't be sure though. They are obviously regulars because they opened the dining room just for them and the chef came in to cook. Must be paying well for all that.'

'What about Naylor?' Emily asked. 'Did he look at you when you went in?'

Steve told Emily the circumstances when he first walked in and how Gwen, the woman behind the bar, had questioned him and how he was able to tell her he was on holiday with his girlfriend. 'She was having some fun trying to embarrass me, but it served our purpose well. Naylor must have heard it all, but I am sure he didn't suspect anything.'

'So, what do we do now?' asked Emily.

'Get something to eat here, mainly so we can extend our stay as long as possible. Then I think we could move on up the street and find a place to wait until they leave the pub. When they come out, I think Harris is the man to follow. We know where Naylor has come from and I would like to see from which stone Mr Harris has crawled. He is a suave looking character, but I bet he's up to his neck in this Naylor business.'

They ordered sandwiches and several cups of coffee, but they eventually decided that they had to move, so they paid the bill and made their way back towards the car park. They were hoping to find a seat they could sit on and play the young lovers again, but the only seat they could find was already occupied by three old men and a dog.

Then Emily noticed the small stretch of road that allowed one hours parking. She stayed and watched to see if either of their two targets were coming up towards her. The streets were beginning to get busy, but neither Naylor or Harris were amongst the crowd. Steve arrived and parked the car next to her. She climbed in, and they waited again.

It was another hour, and Steve was just beginning to think that he would have to move the car when Naylor passed by. He reached the car park and stepped over the low concrete wall, rather than walk the short distance to the gate. The boredom of the hours of waiting faded rapidly to be replaced by excitement. They watched Naylor pull out of the car park, cross the railway lines, and drive off towards Cromer. Harris was about twenty minutes behind Naylor. He was carrying a briefcase and another bag, which looked as though it came from a gift shop. It had three stylised ducks in flight printed on the side of the bag that Steve and Emily could see.

'Someone's going to get a present,' Emily said.

'He looks like a real smooth character. Not at all like Naylor.'

'And I wonder what is in the briefcase?' she said. 'Bags full of jewellery or bags full of money?'

'Could even be some of each, but I would bet it is mainly jewellery. I think the movement of money will be mainly by wire transfers. It's the safest way.'

Harris turned into the car park. Steve drew away from the curb and then also turned into the potholed car park to see where Harris had gone. He was just getting into a large, dark blue, Ford Zephyr. The big car wallowed around on the uneven surface of the car park, as it made its stately way to the exit.

Steve turned their small car around and drove as quickly as he dare towards the road. He didn't want Harris to get too far ahead until they had established which way he was going. As they crossed the railway lines, Harris was turning right, going in the opposite direction to Naylor.

Steve followed a good distance behind the Zephyr. It wasn't moving quickly, so he slowed even more to keep the gap between them big enough for one or two cars to sit behind Harris. Just like Naylor, he drove extremely slowly and carefully.

'He is not going to get caught for speeding,' Emily said.

'No, this is Mr Cautious. I suppose it makes sense if you are driving around with a few thousand pounds' worth of stolen goods.'

They made their way along the coast road, towards Salthouse, where they had followed Naylor the day before. By now two cars had obligingly taken up their positions between Harris at the front and Steve at the back.

They passed the pond at Salthouse, with the usual small number of cars parked on the roadside and families feeding and looking at the birds. They wound their way through Cley-next-the-sea and on towards Blakeney. Cars had joined the growing convoy behind the Zephyr leading the way.

'Why is he going so slow?' Emily said. 'He is almost drawing attention to himself.'

'When I overheard him speak in the pub, he only said a few words, but it sounded a foreign accent, possibly French. If he is used to driving on the right, and with these narrow winding roads, he's probably being extra careful,' Steve said. 'Anyway, he is making life easier for us.'

They drove all the way to Wells before he turned off the coast road and took the main road into the small town.

As a small boy, Steve's mum used to bring him to Wells-next-the-sea as a treat on Sunday afternoons. Wells is an unusual small seaside town in that it has a lovely beach and is also a working port. That was the attraction for Steve. The ships that would come slowly down the winding channel to the quayside were very small when compared with the massive vessels that went into ports like Felixstowe or Hull, but to ten-year-old Steve, they looked massive. He would stand on the quay and look up in awe at the vessels towering over him.

He was so wrapped up in his memories that he almost missed seeing Harris turn left onto a road that led across the back of Wells. A quarter of a mile further on he turned left again. Steve recognised that this led to a lovely green square, with some very grand houses and two very nice hotels. He went past the street and took the next on the left. This brought them into the square on the opposite side to where Harris had gone.

Steve stopped his car, and they spotted Harris just getting out of the Zephyr, which he had parked in front of the garage that adjoined his house. It was by no means the biggest house on the square, but it was still impressive. As he moved towards the front door, a young woman came out to meet him, and they kissed.

'I thought it was his daughter,' said Steve, 'but I think that kiss was a bit too passionate for that.'

'Yes, she did look young for him. Maybe he is not as old as he looks,' Emily said.

'Well, we now know who the present was for. Now we have to find out who he is and where he fits into the business.'

CHAPTER 17

Nick Harris got out of his car, pushing the door closed as quietly as he could. He stepped lightly on the gravel path hoping to surprise Kiki and make her laugh. She loved him playing little tricks like that, and he loved to hear her laughter.

The front door opened and Kiki ran out to meet him. He had only been away for two days, but Kiki always greeted him like this. She was wearing a long white dress and her feet bare. As they embraced, he could tell that she had nothing on underneath. That was her present to him.

'I've missed you, Nick.'

'It's only been two days.'

'Yes, but two days is a long time if you are sitting at home just waiting,' she said.

'I suppose it is,' he said laughing.

'Have you brought me a present?'

'Of course, I have, let's get inside. The neighbours will be watching us.'

Kiki, at 22 years old was 23 years younger than him, but they were both extremely happy. They had been together nearly three years now, and they were closer than ever. He had been the manager of a rubber plantation in Malaya and Kiki had been sent to him as his house cleaner, and her mother would come in to cook his meals every evening.

It was a strange arrangement, but gradually he struck up a friendship with Kiki's mother, who seemed to be pushing Nick and her daughter together. Kiki's father was Dutch and her mother Malaysian. Unfortunately, for the family, their father suddenly decided to go back to the Netherlands, and they never heard from him again. They were left with very little income and were looked down upon by the rest of the villagers, who disapproved of any Malay marrying a Dutchman.

Nick was quick to reassure Kiki's mother that he disapproved of that sort of behaviour from a husband and that he would always take his relationships seriously. Nick realised that getting her daughter married for life to a European would mean her becoming extremely rich, compared to marrying a local man. And, no doubt she thought that would, in turn, bring a certain amount of reward for her family back in Malaya.

He was totally smitten with Kiki; she was beautiful, kind and full of fun. And she seemed to love being with him. She was nineteen, and Malaysian girls grew up much faster than those in Europe. It was only a few months before they were sharing a bed and her mother made it clear that it was with her blessing.

Once again, Nick guessed the reason was that if Kiki got pregnant, he would feel duty-bound to marry her or at least support her. But he didn't care; he wanted to be with Kiki. He was in love with her and felt he was the luckiest man in the world. He had also noted that her mother, who must have been around his age, was also a very beautiful woman. Someone once said that when choosing a wife, always look at what her mother looks like in middle age. So, he did, and the answer was yes, he could live with someone like that for the rest of his life.

His contract came to an end at the rubber plantation, and they came back to Belgium together. He had no job to come home to, but he had plenty of contacts. He put the word out that he was looking for a job and the first person to call him was his old friend Guus Visser. He knew that Guus's businesses were always a little suspect, but he was offering very good money for very little work. There were risks, but most of these were being taken by the couriers. They carried the merchandise across borders, and they were the ones taking the real risk. The money he would get would mean that he and Kiki could live very well and there would be enough to send regular amounts back to Kiki's mother and her numerous brothers and sisters.

Harris also discovered that he had not only brought a beautiful young girl to Europe, but also that she was very bright and learnt to speak, read, and write English in a very short period of time. She had a very good head for maths, which she said she had learned from her father before he deserted them. She had a calm wisdom about her that Harris found very comforting and often discussed business matters with her when he was undecided.

She understood that the business he was engaged in was on the wrong side of the law, but in Malaysia people often had to work their whole life like that in order to survive. She saw no difference, just because she was now in Europe.

'I have cooked you a wonderful dinner to welcome you home. A dinner just like my mother used to make you,' she said.

'I noticed as soon as I walked through the door,' he said. 'The wonderful smell coming from the kitchen gave your secret away.'

'It won't be as good as my mother's, of course, but it will be nearly as good,' she laughed.

After they had eaten, they sat together on the sofa and talked about the day and what they had both done. She had been for her painting lesson that she was receiving from a lady in the town, who was quite a well-known artist. Because it was a nice day they had gone with their easels to the quay and painted watercolours.

'Can I see your painting?' he asked.

'No, it is not finished yet. It needs a lot more work. I didn't even bring it home. What did you do?'

'I had a meeting with Micky,' he said.

She frowned and shook her head. 'I don't like Micky,' she said. 'He is a loud and stupid man.'

'He's not that bad,' Harris said, and then wondered why he was trying to defend him. 'Guus is very cross with him at the moment. He says that Shay and I should get together and talk about what to do in the future.'

'The future of what?' Kiki asked.

'The business and Micky. Guus says that the way he has been acting and showing off in Cromer is putting the whole business, and the people in it, at risk.'

'What can you do?'

'I'll talk it through with Shay, and we will decide. Shay is sensible. We will find a solution together.'

Kiki thought for a while and then said, 'Yes, I am sure that you and Shay will find the way forward. I like Shay. He scares me, but I like him.'

Kiki looked across the room at the briefcase that Harris had laid on the table. 'More beautiful things to send away. Can I look at them Nick my darling?' she asked.

'Yes, you can look, but we must draw the curtains first.' Harris replied.

'When is Franz coming to collect them?' Kiki asked.

'Tomorrow,' said Harris. 'There is a grain ship coming in on today's tide. It is probably moored already. Franz will probably be here at about eleven in the morning, and he won't stay long. He will want to get the goods safely hidden on the ship well before it is due to sail.'

'What does Franz do on the ship?' she asked.

'I don't think he does anything. I think he is a paying passenger. Lots of small cargo ships will take a passenger or two if they have space.'

'He looks like a sailor, the way he dresses.'

'That's so he doesn't look out of place when he comes ashore.' Kiki nodded her understanding.

'If he has gone by twelve-o-clock, I will go to see Shay after lunch. I will suggest that we should arrange to have a meeting with Guus. He will take the decision, so he should share his thoughts with us.'

'I will go and see if I can finish my painting. Then you can see it,' she said.

'If you don't like what Guus says you have to do, would you do it anyway?' she asked and looked into his eyes for a reply.

'If I don't like it, I won't do it,' he said.

'But Guus would not like that.'

'No, he wouldn't. But I have a plan if that happens. You must never tell anyone, but we will go away very quickly. I have been saving up, so we have enough money to start again, somewhere else.'

'Where could we go?'

There are lots of places. Maybe back to Malaya. We could start a business of our own.'

'I would like that. I would like that a lot.'

CHAPTER 18

Emily and Steve had planned a day in Cromer talking to people who might be able to help with their investigation. They felt they knew a lot, but could prove very little. The shop in which Morris Barnack had been murdered remained closed. They had hoped to talk to his widow and add some real human interest to their story, which lacked any real depth at the moment.

There was a notice on the door saying that the shop would remain closed until further notice, but nothing else. The Barnacks lived above the shop, but the people in the shop next door said that they had seen Mrs Barnack go away several weeks ago.

They spoke to the people in all the surrounding shops, but all of them said that she was a very private woman, who seldom came out of the flat unless she was with her husband. As he was such a difficult character to talk to, no one knew much about them. They did not know if she had any relatives in the area, where they came from, or where Mrs Barnack might be now.

Emily and Steve decided to go back to their hotel. When they arrived, Eric was sitting in the reception lounge. He said he had been looking for them, because people in the pubs were talking about a stranger in town, asking questions about Micky Naylor. He explained that he had not seen the man, but a lot of the people who Eric knew felt quite uneasy about this new bloke in town.

They described him as very quietly spoken, but scary. He is above medium height and build, with a short crew cut and piercing blue eyes. He likes to make eye contact with the people he meets. If he asks a question and gets an answer, he will hold eye contact, but say nothing, as if he was expecting them to say more. Most people found this very disconcerting. They found themselves babbling on, repeating themselves because their first answer seemed to be inadequate. Even some of the town's hard men admitted to feeling disconcerted by his presence. They also noticed that he never smiled.

'It's strange that he should turn up now, just after we arrive in town,' said Steve, 'I wonder who he is?'

'I don't know, but his arrival seems to have made people jumpier than ever. Morris Barnack's murder shook people, and I think they were just beginning to get over it when this character arrives and starts asking questions. Apparently, he has a small photograph which he shows to everyone. He says it's a picture of the man he is looking for. One of the blokes in the pub said it looks a bit like Micky Naylor, but it wasn't a very clear image. He seemed to be wearing army uniform, and in the background, you could see a lot of bombed out streets. He said he didn't think it was taken in London; more like somewhere in Europe.'

'Did this bloke have any idea of who he might have been?' Emily asked.

Eric shook his head. 'No, he said he seemed to be someone of authority, but when another one asked him if he was with the police, he just stared at him and shook his head slightly, as if that was the most stupid question he had ever been asked.'

'Does he have a routine?' Steve asked. 'Does he come into the pub at a regular time?'

'No,' said Eric. 'He's only been to the pub I use once, but I know from other people that he has been asking the same questions around other pubs.'

They thanked Eric for letting them know about the newcomer and then decided that what they needed to do was to try and find someone who is close to Naylor, and might be persuaded to talk to them. There was only one possibility Will Bliss and Naylor's wife, Lizzie.

Approaching people close to the heart of the story would be no easy job. They would have to be very careful and sensitive, but the more they thought about it, it was a line of enquiry that they could not afford to ignore. They decided that Steve should casually run into Will. So, Steve set off along the promenade towards the crab boats.

There was no sign of Will when Steve arrived. In fact, everyone seemed to have packed up for the day. Two old fishermen were talking together beside a large pile of crab pots.

They turned towards Steve as he approached. One of them said. 'Don't I know you?'

'Could be,' said Steve. 'This is where I come from.'

'Your Iris's boy, aren't you?'

'Yes, that's right, Steve,' he said, and they shook hands.

'Of course, little Steve. Your mum used to bring you down here to look at the catch, and you just asked question after question. I hope you remember everything we told you.'

'Of course, I do,' Steve laughed.

'Are you back for good or just visiting?' The man asked. Steve was still desperately trying to remember his name. Maybe he never knew it.

'Just a short holiday,' Steve replied. 'I was looking for Will, have you seen him anywhere.'

The man looked around and then he pointed to a white van parked at the bottom of the Gangway.

'I think they're his boots you can see at the back of the van. He has just finished loading.'

'Thanks, it's good to see you again,' Steve called to the fisherman as he walked towards Will. 'I'll come to see you and have a proper chat with you before I leave town.'

'You do that,' he shouted back, 'and give my regards to your mum.'

Will must have heard the shouting because as Steve approached, he looked around the side of the van's open rear door and then came out smiling and shook hands warmly with Steve.

'I heard you were back in town. It's good to see you,' Will said.

'Just here for a week or two on holiday,' Steve said.

Will locked the back door of the van and said, 'I understand it's a working holiday. Eric filled me in with a few details about your visit. I think you might be just the person I need to talk to.'

'Let's get a coffee,' Steve said, indicating the café next to the Lifeboat station. Steve bought the coffees at the counter and carried them to where Will was sitting. It was in a corner, away from the windows with the view over the sea. They were out of earshot of the few customers that were in the café.

'So,' said Will, 'they tell me you are a big-time journalist now.'

'Not quite big time, but we have climbed a couple of steps up the ladder, so we're not grumbling.'

'We,' said Will. 'Who's we?'

'Emily and I worked together on the local newspaper in Peterborough. We got lucky and solved a triple murder case. This brought us to the attention of a few other publications and then we decided to go freelance. It's going okay, and it's why we are here.'

'So is this partnership purely professional,' Will asked with a grin.

'It's both,' said Steve.

'Married?' asked Will.

'No, but we will be soon. And who's supposed to be asking the questions here?'

'You are because I see that you failed to bring beautiful Emily along with you. Yes, I've had a full report from Eric, and he says she is lovely.'

'Eric would think any girl was beautiful if she could cook and do his accounts for him,' said Steve.

'Oh, you've met Susan, have you?' laughed Will. 'But, actually, she is very nice, I could fancy her myself.'

'Will,' said Steve, 'you don't change, do you. You were like this at school. While Eric and I were at football practice, you were off watching the girls playing netball. And you haven't changed one bit.'

'I have actually.'

'What about Super Stud? Where has he gone?' Steve watched Will intently for his reply.

'He's gone for good Steve, honestly. I am in love, and I just don't want anyone else. I've met the perfect girl, and I don't want to lose her. The problem is that she is married.'

'So I hear, and who is she married to?' asked Steve.

'Some guy named Micky,' Will replied.

'Will, it is not just some guy named Micky. It is a highly dangerous nut-case called Micky Naylor that we, Emily and me, are here to investigate. So, it's not just some guy, and if you don't take this seriously, you will finish up in one of your crab pots at the bottom of the North Sea.'

For a moment Will looked shocked, but then nodded his head. 'That's more or less what Lizzie says. She is really scared that he might do something to her, even though their marriage is on the rocks.'

'Listen, Will, persuade Lizzie to come with you and have a meeting with Emily and me. We need her to tell us about Micky's business, so we can understand how it works. She probably doesn't know everything, but almost anything she can tell us will be a help. When the time comes, we will arrange for some professional security people to move in and keep the two of you safe. The magazine we are working for will pay for this, and we will make the arrangements. Do you think you can persuade her to do this? It's really important.'

He nodded. 'I think she will; it's reached a breaking point for her. I'll talk to her.'

CHAPTER 19

Micky had left early in the morning. He was walking, so Lizzie guessed that he was going to London by train. He wouldn't leave his precious Jaguar in the station car park now, ever since someone put a long scratch down one side of the car. He interpreted that, probably correctly, as one of the locals thinking that he was behind the Barnack killing. Lizzie wished that she could blow the car up with him in it, but she knew that she had neither the technical skills or the courage to do such a thing.

Their marriage was a sham now, and she honestly believed that he hated her as much as he hated him. But, no matter how often Lizzie lay in bed thinking of how this might end, she could never see him letting her go. Although she never had anything to do with the running of the 'business', as he liked to call it, she was intelligent enough to see that what he was doing was running a criminal organisation on a large scale. He could dress it up as much he liked, talking about margins and transport costs and returns on investment. If it was such a legitimate business, why did letting an employee go, mean never seeing or hearing from them again? And just like an employee, Lizzie was sure that her destiny also lay in a sudden and unexplained disappearance.

The only person she could turn to in the world was Will. Why did she get poor Will mixed up in this? He lived a very straightforward life and was happy with his lot. She loved him more than she had loved anyone, but she was the one that pursued Will and, as a result, had put his life in danger too.

She had to talk to him today. They could not go on ignoring what might happen. They would have to talk it through and think if there was a way out. She didn't know the answer yet, but maybe talking about it would help find a solution.

She dressed, had some breakfast and drove to her little cottage in Salthouse. It was arranged that Will would meet her there after he had finished work, which he thought would be around 11.30 in the morning. A busy morning meant that it was nearer midday when he arrived.

Lizzie greeted him at the door and the way she clung to him for several seconds longer than usual told Will that Lizzie was in need of some calm, kind words. He could see in her eyes that she was near to tears. They sat on the sofa close together, and he asked her what the matter was.

'I've been thinking about us and what a mess I am in.' her quiet voice breaking as she said the words.

'It's a mess that we are in Lizzie. But you are not alone, and we will find a way.'

'The trouble is that Micky is getting very worried,' she said. 'He is paranoid that people in the town will turn on him, because of what they think he has done. He gets like this when he is under pressure and in this state of mind he can do crazy things. I've seen him in the past. When someone he trusts lets him down, or more likely he just thinks they let him down, that person is seldom seen again. It might just be something that accidentally goes wrong, then someone will, in Micky's eyes, have to take the blame. I'm not saying he has had them all killed, but I'm sure that several people have been murdered. Those that see it coming get out for good and never come back. He is in one of those crazy moods at the minute, and it scares me.'

'Lizzie, I hope you're not going to be cross with me, but there is someone who I think can help us and I would like you to meet him. He's an old school friend of mine and he is now a journalist who specialises in crime. He is in Cromer now, investigating Micky.'

For a moment Lizzie looked horrified at what Will had just said to her. Her mouth opened and closed a few times, but she didn't manage to form any words.

Her silence continued for a few more moments and then it was as if she suddenly saw some hope for the future. Why should she live like this? Micky may be crazy and frightening, but he was only one man.

Will thought he saw a sign that she was at least willing to listen to him.

'You can trust him; Steve is his name. He works together with a girl journalist called Emily. I think they are the only people that can help us and I would trust Steve with my life.' Will could see that she was beginning to believe that there might be a way out for her.

Lizzie whispered very quietly, almost to herself, 'we have to get help from someone. I can't carry on like this. Yes, I'll speak to them and tell them all I know.'

'Can I make arrangements for us to meet here?' Will said. 'Maybe tomorrow afternoon?'

'Yes,' said Lizzie, a new decisiveness in her voice. 'The sooner, the better.'

CHAPTER 20

Guus Visser, Nick Harris and Shay Brady met in a hotel at King's Lynn. It was the only hotel to go to if you wanted the best service and excellent food. Guus always liked to do things properly, including his business meetings. Shay Brady felt slightly uncomfortable in the elegant surroundings, but Nick Harris was very much at home.

Shay and Nick had both arrived early, but separately. Shay had taken the direct route from his house in Cromer, via Holt and Fakenham. Nick, however, enjoyed the ride around the coast from Wells to Kings Lynn, so he had woken early, taken a cup of coffee to his beloved Kiki and then had a leisurely drive.

They both knew that Guus would expect them to be ready and waiting for him in the meeting room. He was a man who hated people keeping him waiting, but he would often turn up two hours late. Shay and Nick would say that was his prerogative; he was the boss. Guus appreciated the professionalism of both Shay and Nick, but their skills were both very different.

Nick was a good businessman and excellent organiser. Over the years he had worked in many businesses and knew how to negotiate with all types of people.

He quickly sensed when a deal was worth pursuing, and when it was time to walk away. He was very confident, but never boastful or overzealous in his sales technique. He also looked the complete, trustworthy businessman.

Shay was like Nick in many ways, even though their jobs were very different. He was a reassuring, confident person, who never spoke unless he had something worthwhile to say. As the fixer in the business, he was always the last resort in solving a problem. He was paid to kill when necessary. Guus believed that Shay always played by that rule. He felt sure that he was a man who did not enjoy killing, but if it was for the good of the company who paid him, so be it.

Guus joined Shay and Nick in the meeting room about thirty minutes after they had arrived. Neither of them asked how he had travelled or if it was a good journey. Guus never revealed any personal information about himself. He turned up when he did, and after the meeting, he would go without a word about what time his train went or when his flight would get him back to wherever he lived.

Guus was, apart from these meetings they occasionally had, a man of mystery. Nick often speculated about where he came from and what nationality he was. He spoke numerous languages fluently and his English, like Nick's, was almost flawless. Guus was always quietly spoken, and generally, he was the voice of reason and common sense.

After the coffee arrived and the handshakes and polite enquiries about everyone's health, the three men sat down at one end of the conference table that ran the full length of the room.

Guus spoke first. 'Thank you for letting me know that the disposal of Arthur has been achieved without mishap Shay. It must have been difficult for you because you had worked with him for some years.'

Shay shrugged his shoulders and said, 'It had to be done. Arthur didn't fit in around here. He got away with things in London, but here he was like a bull in a china shop.'

'Or a bull in an antique shop,' said Guus giggling at his joke, which Shay and Nick dutifully joined in.

'Yes,' said Shay, 'Arthur was making so many wrong calls that he was becoming a liability.'

'And he knew so much about the business; we could not let him walk away. It was the only way,' Guus said. 'But now we come to the main item on today's agenda. What to do about Micky? You go first Shay, you've worked with him for a long time. What is your opinion?'

'For me, it is very much like the situation with Arthur. In the early days, when Micky was working in London, he was high profile, flamboyant and largely respected. In those days if you had money, nobody cared where it came from. In fact, his high-profile worked in our favour. Nobody dare cross him, and it kept a lot of people out of our way, including the police.

'But then, there was a bit of a shakeup, after a few high-profile scams went wrong and Micky suddenly found himself on the police radar. They started to hassle him and make things difficult. It got so bad that we couldn't function properly. And, I understand, that you Guus suggested that we move out of London and run things from up here.'

'Yes,' said Guus, 'when you reported back to me what was happening, I could see we needed to manage the situation and getting out of London seemed to be the best option.

I looked into where we could move and the furthest away from London, yet also having a direct rail link, was up here on the North Norfolk coast. I rang Micky and told him what I thought. At first, he rejected the idea, but then the police raided his house. Luckily there was nothing there at the time, but it scared him into making the move.'

'But unfortunately,' said Shay, 'it made no difference to Micky's lifestyle. It was still very high profile, and that doesn't go down well in Norfolk. They are down-to-earth people, and the locals began to take a dislike to him. One, in particular, Morris Barnack, had a lot to say about Micky's business. That was when he told Arthur and me to go around to his shop and give him a scare. I didn't like the plan, but he wanted it done right away, so I had to do it. I couldn't contact you because there was no time and, in any case, it would have given away the fact that I work for you. And we all know what happened. Arthur went berserk, and Morris Barnack was dead.'

'Yes, I told him he needed to take care of people spreading rumours about him,' said Guus, 'but that didn't mean killing him.

There were lots of other ways to stop Barnack. If Micky had just done a few things for the local community, put some money in for kid's playgrounds or facilities for the old people in the town. He needed to get the community on his side, and they would have turned against Barnack. That is the way to do it. Back home, in the small town where I live, I am the Mayor and have the community on my side.'

Nick and Shay exchanged a quick glance with one another. That was the first time Guus had ever revealed anything about himself. He really must be very concerned about Micky.

Nick agreed, 'Yes, I think that it is very important to be like that and be welcomed by the local people. Kiki does a very good job at making friends, without giving away any information about us. There is a fine line that has to be walked, between having friends, but not close friends.'

Guus nodded agreement with Nick and then said. 'You have worked with Micky for some months now, what do you think?'

'I very much agree with Shay. Micky does not have the subtlety to do these things with the community. He is still living back in the 50s, when crime was black and white before it became a business. People like Micky only survive in the petty crime sector, where they can bully and slap people into agreement. There is no place for that in sophisticated crime.'

'Well,' said Guus, 'I think we are all agreed on that. Micky has to be replaced. What about his wife, will we have to take care of her as well?'

'Possibly not,' Shay replied. 'They are almost estranged from what I hear. She is having an affair with a local fisherman and Micky has a host of girls back in London, who he visits regularly. I think if we put some pressure on Micky, let him know that you are not happy, and he might just take care of her before we have to. He won't want her to ditch him and run off, with everything she must know about the business.'

Nick felt a little unsettled about this talk of taking care of Micky's wife. A scenario of someone wanting to take care of Kiki suddenly flashed into his mind and sent a shock through him. Surely that did not have to happen. She had done nothing to deserve this. And, from what he had heard she certainly got on with the locals. Maybe a little too much.

Whether Guus had seen the look of consternation on Nick's face and guessed what he was thinking, he did not know, but Guus said, 'it may not come to that. If she is fed up with him, she may be a useful ally. Let's wait and see.'

Now Nick worried that Guus might be thinking that he wasn't tough enough for this business. But he shouldn't worry. He had thought about this when he took the job and had put in place an escape plan. The numbered Swiss bank account was set up and growing steadily, and their escape kit was in the safe at home in Wells. He relaxed and concentrated on what Shay was saying.

'Yes, that could be right. I know that he never discussed anything with her, even the move from London. He just told her the removal people were coming the next day and they would do everything. She was already depressed, and that nearly pushed her over into a complete breakdown. Funnily enough, when she got to Cromer, she seemed to love it. But I don't think she ever forgave him. I think they almost live separate lives now.'

Guus looked ready to bring the meeting to an end. 'Okay, I think we agree that Micky is not up to the job, now that times have changed. I will leave it to you Shay to work out a time and place, but please let me know before it happens and if you need any manpower sending over to help. I'll send you anything you want.

'You will then take over running operations in the UK and decide where to be based.'

'Yes, I will keep you posted. I thought that a nice tidy solution would be a suicide. With Micky suspected of being involved in the death of Barnack, with the locals turning against him, the police in London still on his case, and his marital problems, he has plenty of reasons to end it all.

'That sounds good,' said Guus. 'It's the way it should have gone for Barnack, and then we wouldn't have needed to take these decisions.' Shay couldn't be sure if that was partly a rebuke for him as well as Micky. Anyway, in a few days, it all should be over, and he would move out of Cromer to somewhere bigger. It was almost impossible to be anonymous in such a small town.

CHAPTER 21

Will had left a message in reception at the Hotel de Paris for Emily and Steve to come to meet them at Lizzie's cottage at around midday when he would finish work. The last thing they wanted was to arrive before Will got there, so they drove the red Spitfire down to the pond at Salthouse and waited until Will arrived in his white van.

It was round about one-o-clock when he drove past and swung the van onto the little road that ran along the front of the small terrace of cottages. In front of the cottages, there was a large expanse of grass dividing them from the main road. Nosey neighbours were no doubt very familiar with the white van parked outside the end cottage, but the bright red sports car brought a new flurry of twitching curtains.

They walked to the front door and Will let them in. Lizzie stood by his side looking very pale, and her eyes looked as though she had been crying. The introductions done, they moved into the small dining room. The furniture looked new and stylish, with white walls and some nice watercolours of the Norfolk coast. Will and Lizzie sat close together on the sofa and Emily, and Steve took the two armchairs.

'Thank you for agreeing to see us,' Emily said. 'We will quite understand if there are things you don't want to talk about, but without your help, our investigation will take a lot longer, and more people might get hurt. And that includes us, now that people know what we are here to do.' They had discussed who should lead the interview and agreed that Emily should start, using her gentle voice until they could assess how Lizzie was going to react to the questioning.

'I want to tell you everything I know,' said Lizzie very quietly. 'But now I think about it, I know very little. I have lived with him for several years, and he has never allowed me into his other life once. I can see now that I was just his prize pet. I was just there to make him look the part. The successful man with a respectable woman at his side.

'His business dealings and his financial affairs were completely out of bounds for me. And I learned much later, so were numerous other women. It makes me sound like a stupid person, and maybe I am, but I had no experience of people who lie without hesitation. It took me eighteen months to even suspect that anything was wrong with our relationship and then it was another year, and a police raid, before I realised my life was a complete mess.

'So, I am afraid I can't give you a great deal of detail because when I first realised that Micky was tied up with criminals, I became so depressed that I could not think straight at all. It wasn't until we moved to Cromer that I began to see some hope of getting away from him. And I didn't know we were moving anywhere until a couple of days before.

Then I met Will, and that forced me to face up to the fact that I was letting my life go down the drain and doing nothing about it.'

'Okay,' said Emily, 'let's take this one step at a time.'

'What sort of business is Micky involved with?'

'I don't know, but I am pretty sure that it is antique jewellery and art and it's on a fairly large scale.'

'Throughout the UK?' Steve asked.

'Europe as well and probably the USA,' Lizzie said. 'He seems to have plenty of calls from the States, Europe, in fact, all over the world.'

'And Micky was running all this?' said Emily.

'No, just in the UK, which at that time was mainly London.'

'Do you know who was running the whole show?' Steve asked.

She shook her head. 'No, I think he did mention that it was someone he met at the end of the war. What was his name?' Lizzie said to herself. 'I think Micky was in Berlin at the end of the war. He said he knew this man from then. He knew him by just one name. Was it Vince, Vern, no I think it was Victor or something like that. Just the one name. He only mentioned it then because he likes to tell all the girls he meets that he was there when the Allies took Berlin. You would think he stormed in with the infantry, but he was actually in the Army Transport Core, driving trucks of food supplies into the City. I heard him telling a couple of the guys who worked for him how he used the story to get some girl into bed with him. I remember him saying, 'the silly little bitch swallowed it hook, line and sinker. She thought I was a real hero and she was a good shag.

'It was after I realised what sort of person I had married, but I was still shocked by the story and the way they all laughed about it. My father had taught me to have great respect for real fighting soldiers and here was this idiot pretending to be a hero, just to get a shag.'

Emily was beginning to realise just what a traumatic marriage Lizzie had had to endure. She could see what a gentle, trusting girl Lizzie was and completely out of her depth with Micky and the people he worked with. Emily found herself thinking how she would have handled this sort of situation. She would have been wanting to know what was happening from day one; she just could not have kept quiet, she would have challenged what he said. And then she thought, and I would most likely have been dead by now.

Steve stepped in to ask, 'Do you think it was just dealing, or stealing as well.'

'Almost certainly it was stolen. The sort of people Micky worked with didn't look like dealers.'

'Do you know the names of any of these people?' Steve asked.

Lizzie shook her head. 'Only those who worked closely with Micky. There is one called Shay and another called Arthur, but Arthur seems to have gone somewhere because Shay was on his own the last few times he came around to see Micky. It may be that Arthur did something wrong and either had to leave in a hurry, or they have taken care of him. And there was also the mysterious Victor of course, but that was just an alias.'

'Quite a few people disappeared over the years. I often wondered where they had gone, but if I asked he would just say they left. But I can't see that leaving with a reference and a handshake would be possible in that sort of business.'

'Yes, I think you are right,' said Steve with a smile of reassurance.

'How did you come to know him. You don't seem like the sort of person that would mix with his crowd?' Emily asked.

'I can hardly remember. Those days were a bit of a blur. I think a friend invited me to a party to launch some new potential singing star. Flashy Micky often got invited to that sort of bash. With his big expensive cars and a cigar always on the go, he liked to be the centre of the conversation. I was standing drinking Champagne with my friend when he came over and asked me to dance with him. I thought he was going to ask her, and when it was me, I just thought 'great', and said 'yes'.

'In the early days, he was very good to me, but I think even at that time he just wanted someone to give him some respectability. He didn't want to be seen out with his usual flashy tarts. I was a public-school girl, with a father who was a senior officer in the army.

I spoke with the right accent to make him acceptable, and his loudness and coarse language were very popular with the swinging set, who were desperately trying to show how classless they were. In fact, as a pair, we were just what they were looking for.'

'So, when did it start to go wrong?' Emily asked.

'Soon after we got married,' said Lizzie, drawing her hand across her forehead, as if trying to wipe the memory away. 'I was estranged from my family because they didn't like Micky. I wouldn't listen to my father when he told me that Micky was a crook and a 'thoroughly bad lot' as he put it.

'I now know that his changes of mood were because the police were beginning to harass him. They obviously knew that something was wrong, but couldn't prove anything. It deteriorated week by week. Micky ranting on the phone to people and shouting how he was going to 'sort them out'. He was spending more time away, no doubt with his numerous girlfriends, or prostitutes, to give them their proper name.'

'Was this when your depression started?' Steve asked.

'That took a while to start because I was so stupidly naïve that I didn't see where it was all leading. One morning I got up and heard him raving at someone on the phone. When I asked him what was wrong, he just stormed out, and I didn't see him for two days. It suddenly dawned on me what my life had become, and I was frightened to death of him. If I asked for a divorce, he wasn't he just going to say, 'sorry it didn't work out, but off you go'. No, I was going to be 'sorted out', like the people he raved at on the phone. Twenty-five and I felt that I had no future.'

'Coming back to the present Lizzie, do you really think that Micky could kill you?' Emily asked. 'Has he ever threatened you?'

'With Micky, everything he says to me now seems like a threat. That is how he likes to keep control. But he would do it. Or he would certainly get someone to do it, even if he didn't want to dirty his hands. I know him now, and he is a cold-blooded killer.'

'It sounds as if he is the classic combination of a bully and a coward. I understand from things I've read that it is quite common. It seems to be like that, the way he ran away from the police in London, and with the troubles he is now having here in Norfolk. I imagine his bosses, wherever they are, are not happy with the way he is handling things.'

'Yes,' agreed Steve, 'we have to be very careful how we proceed. This has been such a great help to us. Without knowing what was happening, we had nothing to write. But as Emily says, Micky is going to have pressure from all sides, including some from us I hope. And as you have said Lizzie, under pressure, Micky will lash out at anyone and especially people who are close to him.

'For the next day or so, would you be able to carry on living with him?'

Lizzie only hesitated for a second. 'Yes, she said, he is going to London with Shay, to sort out some problems he has there. He said he would be away for two days, that means a good part of the time will be spent visiting his women friends. It also means he will definitely be away for the full two days. Will is taking some time off work so we can be together.'

Lizzie looked at Will and smiled, and he pulled her closer to him. 'I feel safer when Will is around.'

Will gave a nervous laugh. 'Steve will tell you I was no Sugar Ray Robinson at school,' he said.

'None of us were,' Steve laughed, 'that's why Will, Eric and me hung around together. Safety in numbers and the three of us could always outsmart the bully boys.'

'So, the terrific trio are back together again. Eric has been helping us when he can,' said Emily.

'I think it will be more like the terrified trio,' Will said with a smile. 'Yes, Eric told me he was helping out when he could. The word is getting around why you two are here, so be careful. If Micky gets wind of you snooping around, in his current mood, he is likely to blame you for all of his problems.'

Steve explained that they were as careful as they could be and that Lizzie is the one they must look after. He said that they would try and work out a plan that might bring all this to a close in the next few days. He said that he would speak to the editor of the magazine that commissioned them to cover this story. And they know he has one of the nationals lined up to share the story. The newspaper would go to press with it immediately after it was filed. It would be just the headlines and outline of the story for the newspaper, and then the magazine would run a big spread, giving all the details a few days later. Well, at least that is the way he would like to do it, but it is not always the way it works out. All the other newspapers, news agencies and magazines will be sending people up here to grab an angle on the story.

'What we have to do is to get Lizzie into hiding at least a day before the story breaks,' said Steve. He went on to explain that it is likely that the magazine will hire a security company to keep Lizzie and Will safe when the story breaks.

Lizzie and Will seemed to be a little more relaxed, now Steve had explained that there was a plan, but Steve also knew that Will would think that plans can easily go wrong.

'We will all have to be flexible as this investigation progresses, and if we must, we will improvise and change the plan,' Steve said

Will nodded and said that he and Lizzie would keep in touch and he would contact Steve with any new information.

Lizzie said, 'Well, as I said, Micky is going away for two days, so Will is moving in with me at the house on Cliff Drive. We haven't been able to see much of each other for a little while now. And I will feel safer if Will is there with me.'

'Do you think that is wise?' asked Steve. 'What about the neighbours, if they see that Will has moved in.'

'The houses either side are just used as holiday homes. They are only used a few months of the years,' Lizzie said. 'And there is a large hedge at the front, with a gate leading to the cliff walk. Will uses that entrance, and no one can see who comes and goes.'

'What if Micky comes back unexpectedly?' Steve persisted, a little surprised at the blasé way Lizzie was talking about their plans.

'He never does come back early. He will take care of the business matters, and then visit his lady friends. It's always the same.'

'Okay, but with things coming to a head, you have to be more cautious than ever. At least be prepared for the unexpected,' Steve added.

Will smiled lovingly at Lizzie and said. 'We will Steve; I promise I will not let anything happen to Lizzie.'

'Wow, they are in love,' said Emily, as they got back into the Spitfire. 'You could almost feel the atmosphere of love and quite a lot of lust as well. How much time have we got before Eric comes to the Hotel for our meeting about the strange man who has arrived in town?'

'Enough,' said Steve with a knowing smile. He drove far too quickly back to Cromer, but Emily didn't complain.

CHAPTER 22

The telephone rang in the bedroom and woke Steve. For a few moments, he couldn't remember where they were. His scrambled brain worked it out, and he picked up the receiver and said a sleepy 'hello'.

The receptionist said that their guest Eric was waiting to talk to them. Steve asked her if Eric could wait in the lounge, and they would be down in ten minutes. He also asked her to get a drink served to Eric; anything he wanted and put it on their bill.

He looked at Emily, who was still sleeping soundly. He hated to wake her when she looked so peaceful and pretty. But he just had to. If he went down to see Eric on his own, she would be very cross with him. Emily took her work seriously. But they were both in bed with no clothes on. He could certainly get ready in that time, but it's very dangerous to wake a sleeping girl and say, 'put some clothes on and let's get downstairs to meet Eric. You've got eight minutes.'

As she had sparked this impromptu and highly unprofessional moment, he gave her a gentle kiss and quietly called 'Emily'. He tried again, a little louder and then louder still, but there was no sign of life from the sleeping girl. It was no good, he didn't want to get up at all, but he jumped out of bed pulled the covers back and said, 'Eric's here'.

She came to life almost instantly, jumped out of bed and was pulling clothes on rapidly, while he was still trying to find his. There were some on the floor, some on a chair and a shoe under the bed. Five minutes had elapsed, and she was standing by the door, ready to go and watching with some amusement Steve's fumbling efforts to get dressed, while still half asleep.

'Do you want me to go and say that you will be down in a few minutes?' she said.

Steve slumped with relief into the chair and said. 'Yes, if you don't mind, I feel knackered.'

She laughed, 'You were a bit too energetic. I saved some for later; I hope you will be ready by then.' He threw his sweater at her, but the door had closed, and she had gone.

About ten minutes later Steve joined Emily and Eric in the lounge. It was a large, quiet room, with oversized armchairs, a thick pile carpet, and heavy curtains in every shade of red and cream. The size of the room made confidential conversations easy if you spoke in hushed tones. There were only one or two elderly couples in the lounge, enjoying afternoon cream teas, and they had fortunately kept as far away as possible from the three younger people who had already started drinking beer.

'Bloody hell,' Eric said to Steve, 'you look as though you have just run a marathon.'

'I fell asleep?' Steve said.

'You know what it is like when you get a bit older, you have to have an afternoon nap,' Emily laughed.

'It's all right,' said Steve, raising his beer, 'this will bring me around.'

Emily told Eric of their meeting with Will and Lizzie and outlined the plan they had in mind and how they would like to get this finished ready for publication within a few days. Steve said that they had already got enough material, but as it was, only enough to stir the hornet's nest, but not enough conclusive evidence.

Once the story was published, they would pass over what they had collected and let the police take it from there. He supposed that, with what the police had gathered themselves and what they had learned in Norfolk, they might well have enough to get a conviction. But, he told Eric, a crime that goes over international borders is always the most difficult to prosecute.

'How do you think this new guy in town fits into all this? He has caused quite a stir amongst the locals. He has a strange demeanour, and he is scary. Many of them are more concerned about him than this arsehole Naylor.'

Steve, knew Eric very well and he could see that he had a genuine concern about this man. Eric was a phlegmatic character, and it took a lot to get him worried about anything.

'I think Emily and I are going to have to try and track him down, which I know from what you have said is not going to be easy. He could be one of us; a journalist who has been sent to look into this story.'

'But journalists are not usually scary,' said Emily. 'I've known a few cunning and crafty ones, but I have never met a scary one. When you want information from people, it's no good frightening them.'

'What's he asking about?' said Steve.

'I haven't met him, so this is only what I've been told. He has a small photo of a man in army uniform. He shows people the picture and asks them if they know the man. Apparently, it does look like Naylor, but most of the people haven't seen him either, so he's not getting far with that.

'He also wants to know where Naylor lives, who he lives with, who he hangs around with. That sort of thing. My mate, who has spoken to him says he has the manner of a man who is used to getting answers. When he asks a question, if you say you don't know, he stares at you as if you must be lying.'

'Does anyone know where he is staying?' asked Emily.

Eric shook his head. 'I don't think anyone would be brave enough to follow him. There was a rumour going around that he was living rough in the woods, up towards the lighthouse. Some kids said they had found this roughly made shelter, but it was most likely built by other kids. I wouldn't fancy sleeping up there at this time of year.'

'We need to go and look for this guy. Find out what he wants. Who knows, he might know something we don't,' said Steve.

'Rather you than me,' said Eric.

'That's what we are paid to do, and Emily can be pretty scary when she wants.'

For Emily and Steve, the morning after the meeting with Eric was the day that their tactics changed from low profile to meeting the people. They went to the shops and pubs asking anyone who had seen this stranger in town and talking to those who had actually spoken to him, rather than those who were just repeating what others had told them.

Strangely, it was the old people who seemed to quite like the man and the younger ones who were intimidated. Emily put this down to the way the man approached people, probably feeling less need to establish his authority over the more mature citizens than he would with younger people who could have been a threat.

Steve was happy to take Emily's analysis of the different approaches because she was good at understanding peoples' motives. They worked all morning, and by the time they stopped at one of the pubs, two notebooks were nearly full, and Emily and Steve had succeeded in getting a good idea what sort of person they were looking for.

With the picture that the man carried around with him and his authoritative manner, they were both convinced that they were dealing with someone with a military background. They sat in the corner of a very small pub in the back street behind their hotel, thumbing through their notebooks for any other clues. The dark wooden furniture and grimy walls made the corner where they were sitting very dark, and they could only just read their shorthand notes. Each time the door opened and a new person came into the pub they looked up hopefully. Framed in the doorway, with the light shining behind them they could not see what anyone was like until they moved towards the bar. They both knew that the chances of the mystery man walking into this little pub at this time of day was highly unlikely, but they still looked up each time in the hope that it might be him.

They finished their food and decided to go to the woods up on the cliff walk. It only took them about 15 minutes to reach the spot where the houses on Cliff Drive stop and the woods begin. Ahead of them, an undulating grass path led towards the lighthouse, which was set back on a small hill about 300 yards from the cliff edge.

Another fifty yards or so further on, and the path separated. Steve remembered from his childhood that this branch led to the small village of Overstrand. He remembered it because his mother told him that this was as far as he could go. And he did stop at this point if he was on his own, but if Eric and Will were with him, and the weather was nice; well rules are just waiting to be broken. Will was a couple of years younger than they were, but he was always the adventurous one, always wanting to go a bit further, or 'I wonder what's down there?'

But always the practical voice of reason, Eric, would draw the line at anything stupid that Will might suggest. Steve could tell that Will was often just making stupid suggestions to wind Eric up. It seemed strange to Steve that they had hardly changed since those days, and yet he felt a different person completely. He supposed it was because he had left home and they hadn't. Then he looked at Emily, who was walking alongside him, looking slightly nervous at what they might find up here.

'You're very quiet. What are you thinking about?' Emily asked.

'I was just thinking about when Will, Eric and I used to come up here as kids. It's funny that they seem to be very much the same people they were then, but I feel very different. Maybe I'm not all that different after all.'

'The three of you seem to get on well,' said Emily. 'To me, it seems that you haven't been away from each other at all, certainly by the easy way you chat to each other.'

Their conversation was brought to a halt by sounds from the forest. Cracking twigs, branches being brushed to one side and someone shouting. Emily and Steve stopped in their tracks and looked towards the source of the sounds. Suddenly, a Golden Labrador burst out of the bushes, his eyes full of excitement and tongue lolling out of the side of his mouth and spittle flying in all directions. He ran straight towards them, circled them twice and then without losing any speed ran back towards the trees. An elderly man emerged from the trees calling 'Clarence' at the top of his voice. The dog veered away from him but slowed down as he did so until it came to a halt, turned and walked towards the man, its tail wagging happily.

The man called to Emily and Steve, 'Sorry about that, he doesn't usually do that, but he seems a bit spooked today.'

'No problem,' Steve called back to him.

'Apart from a near heart attack,' Emily said quietly, as she smiled at the man.

Steve led them a little further along the path until they came to where it split again, this time running down a steep bank and then disappearing into the trees.

'I think if anyone was living rough, it would be in here.' said Steve. 'This is where it is at its most dense. The trees are left to their own devices here, and no one seems to thin them out.'

He led the way down the bank and into the trees. It was quite a cold, grey day, with a breeze blowing off the sea. Once inside the wood, it was also quite dark. The leaves on the trees were beginning to turn brown, but hardly any were starting to fall. The small amount of light that had been coming down from the grey sky was now largely obliterated. As Emily and Steve's eyes grew accustomed to the gloom, they followed a narrow little track through the wood. In places, nettles almost covered it.

The track split again, and Steve decided to try the branch that went left. After about a hundred yards it stopped at a small clearing. A small fire had burnt out in the centre, and there were beer bottles, cigarette ends and a discarded tube of glue. Also, a condom hung limply from a small dead bush.

'Looks like someone's had a good night out,' said Emily.

'Yes,' said Steve. 'They certainly know how to party around here.'

They retraced their steps and turned down the other path. It was a little wider and obviously a little more used. There was a sudden crack of a twig from somewhere close. Emily let out a quiet little squeak of surprise.

'What was that?' she said in a breathless whisper.

'Just an animal of some sort,' Steve said.

'What sort of animal?' Emily was not a girl of the countryside. She preferred a pavement under her feet and any animals around, out in the open where she could see them.

'There are lots,' Steve answered. 'Foxes, badgers, stoats, hedgehogs, even snakes.'

'Is that meant to make me feel better?' she asked.

'They won't hurt you. They are more afraid of you, than you are of them.'

'I don't think so,' she replied with a nervous laugh.

There was suddenly more scuffling in the undergrowth. Emily looked towards Steve for reassurance.

He laughed. 'It's just the wildlife. We are disturbing them. If the man we are looking for is the sort of person I think he is, he would not be making any noise at all.'

They moved on down the track, Emily keeping so close to Steve that she almost tripped him. Steve stopped suddenly, and she ran into him. She thought he was playing games and was about to complain when she saw what he had seen. It was well concealed from the track and could only be seen through a thin gap between a mass of tree trunks.

There was an old green tarpaulin hanging from a low tree branch. Steve began threading his way through the thick undergrowth, with Emily following a few yards behind and looking decidedly unimpressed with what they were doing. They reached the hanging tarpaulin and saw that it was part of a rough structure, comprising a couple of sheets of plywood, forming the two end walls and the tarpaulin providing the roof and the front wall.

Steve approached very cautiously and lifted a small area of the waterproof sheet, and looked in. 'There is no one here,' he said quickly to allay Emily's fears.

'Thank goodness for that,' she said. 'What on earth were you planning to say to him if he was here.'

'Don't worry,' he said. 'I was pretty certain he wouldn't be here. It's the middle of the day. He can be in much better places than this during the day.'

'Do you think he is a down and out, that can't afford bed and breakfast?' Emily asked, confused as to why anyone who did not have to, would live like this.

Steve laughed. 'No, I don't think that. I think he just can't afford to let anyone know who he is, whatever he's come to do. During the day he can buy food, go into pubs and cafes, even go to see the show on the pier and nobody wants to know his name. If he goes to a hotel of any sort, he has to give his name and sign the register. It's the first thing they ask you to do. And even if he uses an alias, the hotel staff or B&B's owner would be able to give the police a good description. It is a risk he is not going to take.'

'What time do you think he comes back here?' she asked.

'Any time after dark. He'll have his bedroll and sleeping bag. He has put a layer of cardboard on the floor so that he will be quite comfortable. I think he is ex-military. His manner with people, knowing how to gather material together and build a place like this, it all points to an ex-serviceman. I would guess that he has one or two options for sleeping and I think this might be abandoned now and he has found suitable sleeping quarters elsewhere.'

'So, what do we do now?' said Emily, hoping that Steve would say 'let's go back to the hotel'. She had had enough of rustling leaves, breaking twigs and animal noises.

'I think we have done all we can to find out about this guy and in all honesty what we know doesn't amount to much. We might as well go back to the hotel.'

Emily gave Steve a quick kiss and then turned around and began to walk, as quickly as she was able to, out of the woods. All Steve heard was Emily saying, 'I'll go first.' And she was gone.

He took a quick look around but could see that nothing had been left. Not a drink can, or a cigarette end, or even a piece of waste paper. Steve left the little shelter and caught up with Emily just before she reached the edge of the woods.

'You've got an excellent sense of direction,' he said as he caught up with her.

'I have when I'm finding my way out,'

CHAPTER 23

Opportunities for Will and Lizzie to be together seemed to have been few and far between in recent weeks. The truth was that they would only really be happy when they were together all the time. It seemed to Lizzie that Micky was increasingly unwilling to go on his jaunts to London. He seemed to sense danger around every corner and was even jumpy when people came to their door.

It was early afternoon, and Will had parked his van on the Gangway and walked up the cliff pathway from the Council Offices to the high hedge that shielded Lizzie and Micky's house from the numerous walkers that passed by every day.

Today was cold, grey and uninviting. Only the really hardy walkers were out in the chill wind that optimists would call bracing. Will hesitated at the gate, which was set into the hedge and could only be seen when you were a yard or two away. A man went passed, striding along the path with his German Shepherd close by his side. The dog's steps seemed leisurely compared to his master's determined strides. As soon as they were out of sight,

Will opened the gate and stepped into the garden, with its immaculate lawn and neatly trimmed shrubs. The garden continued around one side of the house, and a swimming pool, covered for the winter, was surrounded by neat crazy paving. There was more crazy paving, which formed a broad patio in front of two french windows.

It was early afternoon, but as Will looked through the french windows, he saw Lizzie waiting for him, wearing a long white dressing gown. As he got closer to the window, he could see that she was smiling, in that wistful, mysterious way she had. He could also see that the sheer, white fabric was translucent.

She opened a door, and Will stepped inside. She closed the door and kissed him. Will hesitated, he had come straight from working on the boats and was only too aware that he and his clothes were dirty, smelly and wet. He leant forward to kiss her, being careful not to come into contact with her beautiful, expensive looking dressing gown. But she pulled him close to her, and he felt her body pressing against his grimy jeans and a thick sweater.

'I'm dirty and wet, and I need a shower,' he protested.

'Okay, we will have one together,' she said, leading him up the stairs.

As soon as they reached the bathroom, she dropped her dressing gown to the floor and pulled him towards her.

'You are crazy Lizzie,' he said breathlessly, holding her close to him, feeling the nakedness of her back, as she pressed her body into his thick, rough clothing.

'Why is this crazy?' she asked. 'It's beautiful. Your clothes smell of the sea.'

They were soon together in the shower and then into the bed. Their love-making was intense, almost desperate. When, at last, it was over they both lay still and quiet.

'I take it that Micky's not at home then?' Will said, and Lizzie laughed with happiness.

Unsurprisingly, they both felt hungry, so Lizzie made some sandwiches, which they ate, sitting side by side on the sofa, listening to Lizzie's favourites, the Beach Boys. Will was more of a James Brown man, but if Lizzie liked the Beach Boys, so did he.

They talked about what they might do after Lizzie had divorced Micky. How he might react to her telling him she wanted a divorce. Sitting discussing it with Will, made everything seem possible, but Lizzie knew that as soon as she was on her own again, very different thoughts would come into her head.

The fear of violence was never far away, even though Micky had never actually physically attacked her. His psychological attacks on her, particularly during her depression had been brutal. She didn't know how she had survived them, or even if she had survived them. Perhaps they had just pushed her over the top and into a euphoric state of happiness. Was it just an illusion? Was she really that happy?

Then she looked at Will who was talking to her about how they could start a business together, selling fresh crabs directly to hotels and restaurants. Will was so positive about their future and the happiness it could bring. No, it really was going to be okay. All she had to do was survive.

After the discussions about their future and watching some dreadful early evening television, Lizzie began to think about Will coming in through the French doors and the powerful urges that overtook them both. Would it be silly to suggest they went upstairs now, at 8.30 in the evening? Would it be a disappointment? Could the same magic be re-created? Will might be tired; he had been up early this morning, done a day's work and then all that happened when he got here? But, wasn't he called Super Stud by the other fishermen? Time to put it to the test, she thought with a smile.

'This television is not very good, is it? Perhaps it's time to go to bed,' she said.

He smiled. 'I thought you'd never ask.'

Having lived so long with Micky, Lizzie had learned that in his line of work, security was important. She went around and locked all the doors and windows. Then led Will upstairs to the bedroom.

Will kept a few items of clothing in Lizzie's bedroom, so he could get out of his working clothes and be comfortable during his visits. His jogging bottoms and polo shirt were also easily removed.

Lizzie had started by removing the polo shirt as they walked up the stairs. As they walked into the bedroom, she pulled his jogging bottoms down. He staggered across the floor, laughing and trying to dislodge the trousers which were clinging to his ankles.

That was when the doorbell rang. One second they were like a couple of kids, the next a blanket of fear had fallen on them.

'Who's that at this time of night?' Will said, sitting on the bed with his trousers around his ankles.

Lizzie thought for a moment and then said, 'I bet it's that little man from the Church with his raffle tickets for the old folks Christmas party fund. I didn't have any money when he called, and he said he would come back.' She felt relieved that she had remembered.

'Can you take a look at him from the window on the landing,' Will said.

Lizzie ran to the window. 'I can't see him properly, but it looks like him.'

The bell rang again, this time for longer.

She ran back into the bedroom, rummaged around in her bag and took out her purse. She took a pound note out and ran downstairs. The bell was ringing again.

Lizzie opened the door and began to apologise, but stopped mid-sentence. 'Oh,' she said, I thought you were the man from the Church.' She smiled nervously.

The man was medium height, with close cut hair, weather-beaten face and piercing blue eyes. The way he just stood calmly, weighing her up, made her even more nervous. At that moment, she suddenly thought I know why you are here. Micky has sent you to kill me. Of course, that is how it is going to end. She had often wondered how Micky would do it and now she knew. True to form, he has sent someone else to do his dirty work.

'I've come to see Micky Naylor,' he said quietly and without any emotion.

Lizzie was so pleased to hear those words; she smiled again. 'I'm sorry, but he's away, in London I think.'

'And I think he's here. I've been watching. There is a man here, isn't there.'

'No,' said Lizzie, 'there's no man here.' She immediately regretted what she had said, but it was too late.

The man stepped quickly forward, and a hand clasped Lizzie around her neck so quickly that she had no time to call out. He propelled Lizzie backwards into the hall pushing her back towards the stairs. He stopped when her back came up against the bannisters and then pressed her neck until she began to fight for breath.

'Tell him to come down,' the man said.

Upstairs Will had heard a scuffle below and was frantically looking for a weapon he could use. Will was strong, and he could defend himself in a set-to at the pub. But this intruder was bound to be a professional, so he needed a weapon.

'Please come down Will,' Lizzie said as loud as possible with a hand squeezing her windpipe. 'Please, now.'

All Will could find was an umbrella. It would have to do, no matter how ridiculous it looked. He had pulled his trousers up as soon as the sound downstairs began to indicate trouble. So, with an umbrella in hand, wearing baggy trousers and bare-chested, he tried his best to look threatening as he descended the stairs.

As soon as he saw Will, the man let go of Lizzie. She sank slowly to the floor, coughing and spluttering for air.

'If you've hurt her, you're in big trouble mate.' Will knew the words sounded ridiculous as soon as he said them.

The man just stood and watched him walking cautiously down the stairs. Suddenly Will let out a blood-curdling yell and lunged at the man with his umbrella. The man ducked under the flailing umbrella and delivered two quick blows to Will's neck.

Lizzie looked in horror as Will collapsed to the floor and lay still. 'You've killed him, you bastard, you've killed him. You didn't need to do that. He was only trying to protect me.'

'Shut up,' the man said. 'He's not dead.'

'How do you know?' said a tearful Lizzie. 'You can't be certain.'

'Yes, I can. Feel his pulse if you don't believe me.'

Lizzie, still crying, climbed to her feet and walked to where Will was lying. She took hold of his wrist placed her fingers on it. 'There's no pulse,' she screamed at the man. 'You have killed him.'

He walked over and bent down and felt Will's neck. 'There's a pulse. He'll be okay in a while.'

'Why did you have to do that?' asked Lizzie.

'I did that to prevent him getting hurt. If I hadn't, I might have had to kill him. It was for his safety.'

Lizzie looked at the man and shook her head. 'He was only trying to protect me. You come bursting in here like you did. What do you expect? People get scared.'

'So, where is your husband?'

'He is supposed to be in London, but who knows where he is. He could be anywhere. Wherever he is, I would be the last person to know. He tells me nothing,' she sobbed and stroked Will's hair as he lay unconscious on the floor.'

'When your husband comes back I want you to give him a message,' the man said to Lizzie, who was still crying quietly next to Will.

'Are you listening, because it's important.' Lizzie nodded her head and looked over to where he stood. 'I want you to tell him that I'm coming back to put things right for what he did in Berlin after the war. Have you got that?'

'Yes, but I don't understand it.'

'You don't have to, just give him the message exactly as I told you.' Lizzie looked confused.

'Look, go and find a piece of paper and a pen and come back here.' Lizzie wanted to do as she was told, but she didn't want to leave Will. 'Go and get the paper and pen and I'll make sure your boyfriend is okay.' He didn't raise his voice or look angry with her, but she got unsteadily to her feet and walked slowly into the kitchen, almost as if she was in a bad dream.

When she returned a few minutes later, he had propped Will against the wall in a sitting position. The man was gently slapping his face and Will was making small moaning noises as if he was beginning to come round.

The man stood up and repeated his message to Lizzie. She felt dizzy and could hardly comprehend what he was saying. But he was very calm and precise in giving her the message, and after she had finished, he checked it to make sure she had written it correctly.

'You give that to him as soon as he comes home,' he said to Lizzie. 'And look, your boyfriend's looking a lot better now. Sorry if I have caused you any inconvenience, but that message is important to me, so make sure he reads it.'

He opened the door and was gone.

It was about twenty minutes before Will had been able to stand up and walk to a chair in the kitchen. Lizzie got him some water and gave him two aspirins to take. Will was looking very sorry for himself and embarrassed that he had not been able to protect her. Lizzie didn't care about anything, except that Will was alive and as well as can be expected in the circumstances.

Will wanted to call the police, but Lizzie felt that might make things more complicated. Admittedly, she was not the one that had been rendered unconscious by a stranger who had just forced his way into the house, but that wasn't why she didn't want to call the police. She saw the situation in an entirely different light to how Will viewed it.

If this man had taken the trouble to track Micky down for something that happened 18-years ago, he was presumably not going to shake his hand and say, 'nice to see you again'.

By the look of the man and the tone of his message he was here to do something far more drastic and that meant that Micky might be distracted enough to turn his attention to self-preservation, rather than planning her demise.

'This could work for us,' she said. 'I know it's a shock now and that you could have been killed, but now it's over, this could save us from Micky. If this man really is a threat to Micky, and he certainly looks capable to me, it might be a distraction that works in our favour.'

Will was still looking groggy. 'It could be a way out,' he said in a husky whisper.

Lizzie held Will close to her, 'Let's hope that something good can come from this. We should go to bed now and see what we think in the morning. I can hardly think straight at the moment, and you must be feeling terrible.'

CHAPTER 24

The following morning Emily woke before Steve, but she must have disturbed him because as soon as she pulled the curtain back and looked out of the window, Steve mumbled, 'What's the weather like?'

'Foggy,' said Emily. 'No, I think it's a fine drizzle. You can only see as far as the end of the pier. I hate days like this. Nothing good ever happens in this sort of weather.'

Steve got out of bed and immediately sat down. This was his morning ritual, he took things very slowly for about ten minutes, and then he was okay. So, for ten minutes Emily would rush around and get ready and then she could sit in comfort at the dressing table, while Steve occupied the bathroom. Then, like a well-drilled team, they were ready to go to breakfast at the same time. It was almost eight-o-clock when they sat down for breakfast, and half an hour later, they stood up to leave. The dining room overlooked the seafront and the pier, and as Steve looked outside, he noticed Will sitting on the wall. Normally, at this time, Will would be busy, getting the boat ready to go out to the pots, or he would be sorting through the day's catch.

'Will's outside. I think he might be waiting for us.' Steve said.

Emily came to the window to see for herself. 'I thought he said he was having a couple of days off work, while Micky was away.'

'Yes, I think he did. I wonder what he wants?' said Steve. 'Let's get our coats and go and see. He might have some news for us.'

As soon as they approached Will, Emily and Steve could see that something was wrong. Will wasn't his usual smiling self, and as they got they got closer, it was clear to see that he was unwell.

'What's the trouble Will?' Steve asked. 'You look terrible.'

'Yes, we had a visitor last night. It must be this man that everyone is talking about. We don't know what to do. I told Lizzie I would sort it out and went down to the boat thinking that doing the ordinary routine things might clear my mind. But it hasn't, so I thought I would come and tell you. Maybe you can help.'

'Yes, of course, we can,' said Emily, always the optimist. 'Come to the hotel and sit with us.'

'No, I can't go in there in my working clothes,' Will said. 'There's a little café on the front. It will be open now.'

They walked down the zig-zag path from the hotel and down to the promenade. Emily noticed how pale and drawn Will's face looked. She couldn't imagine what had happened to bring about such a change in him.

Steve bought them coffee and took them to a table near the window. The early morning drizzle had persisted and covered the outside of the window and inside, a layer of condensation prevented anyone being able to recognise them. As the café counter was situated right at the back, even though the place was small, they would be able to have a conversation without being overheard.

As soon as they were seated, Will began to relate what had happened.

'He came about 8.30 or maybe 9.00. He just rang the bell and forced his way in. I was with Lizzie, in their house on Cliff Drive. He grabbed her by the throat and asked her where Naylor was away. She told him he wasn't there, but he must have seen me come in and thought it was Naylor. He told her to tell me to come down. I tried to find a weapon in the bedroom, but the only thing there was a bloody umbrella. I must have looked a real tool coming down the stairs with a green and white umbrella in my hand. It must have looked like the start of a Gene Kelly movie.' Will shook his head in disbelief of what had happened.

'Anyway, I charged at him, waving the umbrella about, because he had still got Lizzie by the throat. He immediately let go of her and the next thing I know I am waking up about twenty minutes later. Lizzie is crying and trying to write a message down that this guy is dictating to her. He is chilled out, all very calm and friendly now. Obviously, he got what he wanted.'

'What did the message say?' Steve asked.

'I didn't read it, but Lizzie said it was about him coming for Naylor to put right something that had happened in Berlin at the end of the war.'

'Well, he's obviously not a man to forgive and forget.' Said Steve 'It must have been something nasty that happened in Berlin, but if Naylor was involved, that goes without saying.'

'Lizzie was convinced that the man had been sent to kill her and that he was one of Micky's hit men. But, it turned out that Micky was the target. She thinks that this might be a good thing for us and that this bloke could be a distraction for Micky and allow Lizzie to get away.'

'I think she's right,' said Emily. 'There is only so much he can concentrate on at the same time, and someone from the past with a king-size grudge would definitely get Micky's full attention. Nearly twenty years with that eating away at him; that is a lot of time to build the hate.'

'So, what do we do now?' said Will.

'The first thing is to make sure that Lizzie gives Naylor the message as soon as he gets home, and then get out of there immediately afterwards. She has to tell him about how frightening it was and what a crazy man he seemed to be. We need to speed up Micky's panic to hysteria level.'

'Okay, I'll tell her what you said. I think that is how she saw the way forward, so I don't think there will be any problem,' Will said.

'Emily and me need to find out who this mystery man is. Sooner or later he is going to show himself in town again, and we might be able to do a deal with him,' said Steve. 'He is obviously no friend of Naylor, so at least we are on the same side. We might be able to offer to tell his story, alongside revealing Naylor's other exploits.'

'It's getting close enough to talk to him before he disappears again' said Emily. 'He sounds like a person who acts first and asks questions later. So, if we are not careful, we could get the same treatment as Will.'

'He certainly is a difficult person to deal with. He is totally focussed on what he has to do,' said Will, 'but he is always in control of himself. No unnecessary violence, but he is going to get what he wants, whatever that is.'

'Yes, we're going to have to move things forward as fast as we can. I'll ring our editor and see if we can get things moving over the next few days. If we can agree on some copy deadlines with him, I think Emily and I have got enough to go to press with a decent story. And, if anything newsworthy happens in the meantime, so much the better.

'I'll also bring up the security issue for you and Lizzie, and for Emily and me for that matter. Normally, we would go to the police, but we know there is at least one leak there, so we can't afford to take any chances.'

'Okay,' said Will, 'I'll go and talk to Lizzie and tell her what you are going to do.'

'And make this the last time you two meet at the Cliff Drive house. It's too risky.'

Steve went up to the bedroom and called Martin Yates, the editor of the magazine they were working for. He sounded relieved to hear from Steve, and he guessed that Martin had been worrying that they had spent a lot of time in Norfolk and might have discovered that there was no story at all.

Steve described the difficulties they had at first, but to allay Martin fears, he told him the break-through that they had when Naylor's wife agreed to tell them everything she knew. Martin sounded very relieved and began to congratulate Steve and Emily on their good work.

'Unfortunately, it is not quite as straightforward as it sounds. She is very straight with us. She knows very little details and only a few of the people who work for Naylor. But together with the information you had before, I think we have got a strong story now. It completely fits with what you have been told.

'She was certain that it is jewellery, and maybe art, which has been stolen in one country and is being smuggled out and sold somewhere else. She was also of the opinion that the real control of the operation was from somewhere in mainland Europe.'

'Is this girl mixed up in all this. Is she trying to buy her way out?' Martin asked, obviously thinking that the cost of this would be going up if she wanted a fee for her story thought Steve.

'No, it's not like that at all. She and Naylor live separate lives now. They are like chalk and cheese. She is public school educated, daughter of a high-ranking army officer and he is an uncouth yob.'

'How the hell did they get together?' said Martin.

'You know how it is these days,' said Steve. 'All sorts of up and coming working class lads find a way to make a fortune. Actors, singers, fashion designers, photographers, all sorts making a fortune and being welcomed with open arms by the posh young things who want to show how classless they can be. And I am pleased they are because I wouldn't have got this far if the old school tie brigade were still keeping us in our place.'

Martin laughed, 'Yes, that goes for me too. But this couple does seem to be at the absolute opposite ends of the spectrum.'

'Yes, Lizzie is a nice, kind girl, but I think a few years ago she had her head in the clouds, probably getting in with the wrong crowd and maybe smoking things that she shouldn't. I think her father saw through Naylor from the start, but the more he protested, the more determined she was to marry him.'

'Sounds like there could be a whole series of spin-offs from this,' Martin said. 'Would she play ball and let us tell her story.'

'I think she would. She wouldn't want anyone to go through what she has.'

'It's all sounding very positive, but there has to be a downside,' Martin said.

'Yes,' Steve agreed, 'there is. I think we may need some security as this nears the end. I can't go to the police, for various reasons, and we certainly would need someone to find a way to keep Lizzie safe, because any number of people could be after her when it comes to a head.'

'No, that's fair enough, and it sounds as though she could provide us with some good, controversial stuff.'

'Okay, now that things are moving I will keep in touch with you every day,' Steve said. That way we can be prepared when we have to bring the heavies in.'

'Give my regards to Emily,' Martin called as he rang off.

CHAPTER 25

Nick Harris called Shay late in the evening, just after Shay got back from the pub.

Shay had found a pub on the outskirts of town that several Irish lads used. They were an odd assortment, who spoke very little about themselves in the present day, but a great deal about when they were young in Ireland. Some were from the South and some from the North, some Catholic some Protestant, but that was never discussed either.

They were a bunch of middle-aged men reliving their childhoods. The strange thing was that growing up in Ireland at that time was tough. There was little work for their parents to do, and with large families, it meant a constant struggle. But somehow, this little group found comfort in talking to each other about their hardships. At times, it became a competition about who was the poorest, and then it could get heated. But generally, it was pure nostalgia and a great deal of humour.

For Shay, it was a sanctuary and somewhere safe to talk. Nobody asked what he did for a living. It filled a hole in Shay's life. He had always worked with a partner since leaving the Army and starting work with Micky and then Guus.

Having to get rid of Arthur, necessary as it was, left a gap in Shay's life. Like any good Irishman he liked to talk, but in his business, you had to be careful in what you say and what you do. Unfortunately, Arthur never learnt when to be quiet and, when threatened, he would inevitably overreact.

It was only a few days after their meeting with Guus, so Shay was surprised by the call from Nick.

'Can we meet tomorrow morning?' Nick said. 'Guus has had an idea about the little problem we need to solve. He asked me to run it passed you, and we shouldn't speak about these things on the telephone.'

'It's okay with me, just say when and where.'

'Come to the main car park at Sheringham. I'll park right in the centre, and you come up alongside. We can talk in my car and then we won't be overheard or even seen together. Let's make it nine in the morning, and that guarantees that it will be quiet.'

When Shay went out to his car in the morning, it was just beginning to rain. By the time he was joining the coast road to Sheringham huge drops of rain and hailstones were beating on the roof of his car.

He was glad he had set off early. It was only a short distance to Sheringham, but the roads were turning into torrents of water several inches deep. As he approached Sheringham, the rain abruptly stopped, and as he turned into the car park, the sun came out.

He was there first, but only just. A few moments after he had stopped, he saw Nick's dark blue Ford Zephyr turn sedately into the car park. It was not a pretty car, Shay thought, a bit like an aircraft carrier on wheels.

Shay got out of his car and slid into the big Zephyr. They shook hands.

'Hello Nick, you wouldn't believe the rain I've just come through, and now the sun is shining.'

'I could see the cloud,' said Nick. 'Thought it was coming my way, but then I saw a rainbow, and it was gone. Very spectacular.'

'Okay Nick, what's the problem?' Shay asked.

'There's no problem at all. Guus rang me to make a suggestion.'

Shay laughed. 'Come on Nick, you know as well as I do that if Guus makes a suggestion, we all salute and say 'yes, sir'.'

Nick had a little chuckle at what Shay had said. 'No, no, he didn't mean it like that. After he left our meeting, he thought that we were putting too much on you. You had been asked to deal with Arthur, who you had worked with for many years, so that couldn't have been easy. Now we are asking you to deal with Micky, who has been your boss for even more years. We shouldn't be putting everything on you. It should be shared.'

'It's not a problem,' said Shay, thinking that they thought he was going soft.

'He knows that, but also I think his idea is a good one. You will be in charge of the set-up and everything that goes with it. You are the one who knows Micky and the way he thinks and works. So, you set it all up, but he will send two of his best men, to make the kill and stage the scene to look like a suicide. When the kill is made, you will be miles away in London, with a rock-solid alibi that will take all suspicion away from you.'

'You have to hand it to Guus,' said Shay, 'he knows the way to do things properly. Leaves nothing to chance.'

'They will contact you and will be here in the next couple of days. It may be a bit sooner than that. You see what Guus had done, don't you, he has taken the way we work in the mainstream business and turned it into a method of getting rid of Micky now that he has become a liability. It is, as you say, a very sensible way to go.'

'What nationality are these guys. Do they speak English?'

'I don't know the nationality. It doesn't matter to us; nobody knows Guus's nationality. Nobody knows mine.'

'Surely you are English with a name like Nick Harris,' said Shay with a smile.

'You mean I didn't fool you?' Nick laughed heartily. 'I thought I had fooled everyone.'

'Am I the only one who is happy to say I'm Irish.'

'You can say that because everyone loves the Irish. The Irish are welcome everywhere.'

'I'm afraid some of us are not even welcome in Ireland but don't let's go there.'

'Well, whatever the nationality, these two both speak English, one better than the other apparently. But even if they can't say much they will understand you. Make the handover as quick as possible. Brief them on what should happen and then get off on your planned trip to London. The killing should be planned for only four or five hours after the briefing. Then they will leave the country.'

'I do know, and I guess you do as well, that we will have to move operations away from here. So, be giving it some thought. We need somewhere bigger and busier than here, but it still needs to be away from London. Maybe about one and half hours by train, something like that.'

CHAPTER 26

Micky returned to the house a day later than expected. Lizzie had stayed in yesterday afternoon and most of this morning. She was taking Steve's advice and cutting out the risks. She watched Micky walking down the driveway and thought how old he was beginning to look. The pressures were building on him, and as usual, he would respond badly. He would be looking to pick a fight with her. He always did when things weren't going his way. He would lash out at anyone who was close to him.

He looked like thunder as he came towards the front door, she stepped back into the shadows so he couldn't see her watching him. As he fumbled his keys into the lock, Lizzie scuttled through to the kitchen and began to make some coffee. But she couldn't be too nice, or he would wonder what she was hiding. After almost a year of bickering and depression, she had to walk a fine line between hate and tolerance.

He burst into the house as if it were a police raid and stood looking around.

'Lizzie', he bellowed, 'where are you?'

'In the kitchen,' she answered in a flat voice. 'I'm making coffee.'

'Good. I'll have one.'

She said nothing but started to pour coffee into a cup.

'I dropped in on Shay, and he tells me there are a couple of fucking nosey journalists hanging around and trying to get a story about us. And I don't mean just you and me, the whole bleedin' operation.'

Lizzie carried his cup of coffee through and put it in front of him, but still said nothing.

As she walked away, he said, 'Well, aren't you going say anything. Did you know about them?'

'Yes, I had heard, but only through friends I've made, telling me the gossip around the town.'

'Well, you could have told me. I would have soon put a stop to their snooping.'

'I didn't know if it was true. It could have just been gossip and nothing more,' she said and continued walking back to the kitchen.

'Well it's not, and you'd better be careful if you see them around. I've told Shay to take care of them.'

'What, the same way he took care of Morris Barnack?' As soon as she had said the words, she regretted them. She was mad, he'd only been in the house five minutes, and she started him off again.

He came storming into the kitchen, his face set in a mask of anger. He got close up to her, grabbed a handful of the jumper she was wearing and pulled her towards him until their noses almost touched.

'Don't you ever say that again, you stupid little whore. I never lifted a finger against Barnack. It was a burglary that went wrong. Do you hear me? You're very lucky that I've put up with your nonsense as long as I have.'

Lizzie burst into tears just at the sheer ferocity of Micky's attack on her. She felt spots of spittle landing on her face and lips.

'And let me tell you, I have had enough of it now. Do you hear me?' he screamed at her and slapped her hard across the face twice. 'You have been a complete bitch to me, and after all, I've given you.' He slapped her twice again, this time not as hard as the first two, but hard enough to jolt her head backwards.

Lizzie was just hanging limply in front of him, his hand still clinging to the jumper, which was now right under her chin. She was just sobbing now, not asking him to stop or pleading with him. Her stretched jumper was now supporting her under each armpit, leaving her exposed and terribly frightened. She knew that the only way to stop him was to say nothing and not to fight back.

At last, he let go, and she sank to the ground still sobbing. She sat in a crumpled heap on the floor; her long slim legs had folded underneath her. Her nose and eyes were dripping with tears and emotion. She noticed that her small breasts were still on view and pulled her jumper down to cover herself.

'I'm not going to put up with your behaviour any longer, whoring around the town and giving me lip every time I come home. This is your final warning, and if I find out that you have been talking to those fucking journalists, you are a dead woman. Do you hear me, a dead woman?'

Lizzie lay on the kitchen floor thinking what to do next. After a while, she picked herself up and walked towards the bedroom. Micky watched her as she climbed the stairs, but did not speak. She went into her bedroom and locked the door. She walked over to her dressing table and pulled the drawer open. Inside lay the message, written by her at the instruction of the stranger the other night.

She looked down at the scruffy piece of paper, with her nervous scribble on it. The words looked as though they had been written by a seven-year-old. But the message brought a smile to her face. Okay, Mr Naylor, I was saving this for a better occasion, but you might as well have it now.

She changed into her best trouser-suit and shoes. Her face was a mess from the slapping, but she did her best to cover it with some make-up. Her case was already packed in the car. She had already thought about what might happen if she had to make a quick exit. That was last night; she didn't expect to be using it today.

She took the message from the drawer, read it again and smiled. She looked around the room to check that she had not missed anything that she might need. The stuffed toy tiger had been a good friend in her dark days of depression, but it would look too obvious if she carried that out through the front door. And she might be able to get him back someday in the future.

She walked downstairs as confidently as she could make it look. Micky was sitting looking gloomily at a newspaper.

'Where are you going?' he asked.

'We need some groceries,' she said. 'Do you need anything; the whisky and brandy are getting a bit low.'

Micky sat and stared at her as if he was trying to work out what she was up to. Then he said, 'You'd better get some then, didn't you?'

'Okay,' she said. She hoped that he was thinking that his slapping had brought her into line. He often used to say about people, that they'll be all right after a good slapping. 'I won't be long.'

She reached the front door and laid the note down on the table, which formed part of an umbrella stand. 'By the way,' she said, 'a man called yesterday to see you. He left a message for you; it's on the umbrella stand.'

She instantly had his attention, 'What man, who was it.'

'I don't know, but the message is there.' She waved a hand at the umbrella stand and then opened the door and left.

She got into her car and started the engine. Micky came running out waving the note at her. She opened the window just enough to speak.

'What's this all about? Who was it? What does he want?'

Lizzie shook her head. 'I've no idea. He said you would know what the message meant. See you later,' and she drove off.

CHAPTER 27

Lizzie drove triumphantly out of the driveway and down the road towards town. But almost instantly a realisation of what she had done swept into her mind. Steve would not have had time to arrange any security for her, and that would mess up his timings for breaking the story. If only she had kept quiet about Barnack, but what Micky had done had been smouldering inside her ever since it happened. She was suspicious that Micky was behind it, and now he had proved her right with that outburst. But that didn't help the plan that Steve and Emily had worked out, for her benefit. She had let them down badly and needed to talk to Will.

She drove to the Gangway and parked at the top of the hill. She looked down to the beach, but all she saw was a couple of men working on a rusty old tractor. All the boats were out at sea. She turned her car around and drove back and parked a short way along the Runton Road, which was only a small distance from the Hotel de Paris.

Lizzie checked to make sure that no one was watching the hotel entrance. She thought that now Micky knew about Steve and Emily, he might send someone round to watch the main hotels.

She knew that he had made a few contacts in town, for his own security, but more likely he would ask Shay to come looking for them. When she didn't return from her shopping trip, he would almost certainly add her to his wanted list.

As far as she could see, there was no one watching, but she only had a few spy films that she had watched, to have any idea of how to spot someone on surveillance duty. She stood and watched, but people were looking at her because she looked so out of place. Her flashy trouser-suit was made to be worn on the Kings Road in London, not the seafront at Cromer. With her sunglasses on to hide the bruise marks made by Micky, and her tall, slim build, she looked like a model or a film star.

She began to feel very self-conscious and decided to go into the hotel in the hope that Steve and Emily were there. Walking into the reception foyer, she felt all eyes turn towards her, and she made her way to the desk, where a lone young girl was writing in a large book.

'I wondered if two friends of mine who are staying here might be in the hotel.' she asked quietly, not wanting any of the people sitting around in the foyer to hear.

'What are their names please?' the girl asked.

'I only know their first names I'm afraid. We only just met a few days ago. They said to drop in if I was in town. Their names are Emily and Steve. They are quite young,' added Lizzie. There couldn't have been anyone in the foyer younger than sixty.

The girl smiled. 'Yes, they are staying with us.' The girl looked at the keys hanging from a board behind her. 'No, I'm afraid they are out at the moment. Shall I tell them you called or would you like to wait?'

'I'd like to wait please, but I have some confidential papers to go through. Is there anywhere that I could sit in private?'

'Yes, we have a small office you can use, just down that corridor, on your right.' The girl pointed to an opening in the wall, almost alongside the reception desk.

Lizzie thanked the girl and settled herself into the little office. The décor was predominately red, as was the rest of the foyer. There was one desk, one chair, a telephone and a large blotting pad, which also had gold edging. There was a small pile of hotel letterhead paper on the desk, and Lizzie took a few pages from the pile and placed them in front of her. She rummaged in her bag for a pen and tried to think of something to write so that her request for privacy made sense.

She began to make a list of the times that Micky had abused her mentally and made her feel worthless. After some careful thought, she remembered at least eleven times when he had overstepped the mark and driven her deeper into her depression. And there were many more, but only once was it was a physical attack. The one this morning. It wasn't life-threatening, but it was very painful and frightening. What Lizzie had learnt about herself was that she could stand up to a physical attack, better than an attack on her mind. Right at this minute, she felt strong and pleased with herself that she had had the guts to walk out on him. Maybe because this time it was different. She had people who cared about her and would look after her. Will, Emily and Steve would be there for her, no matter what, she told herself. But the dark shadow of Micky still hung over her. She was not safe yet.

CHAPTER 28

Steve and Emily had experienced a frustrating day trying to track down this man, who had given Lizzie and Will such a hard time the other night. They searched everywhere and asked everyone who could be helpful, but no one had seen him or could even guess where he might be. They decided to go back to the hotel and concentrate on getting the stories that needed to be completed to draft stage, even though there were still some gaps to be filled.

Cindy, the girl on the reception desk, looked particularly happy to see them as they walked in through the revolving door. As they walked over to her, she could barely keep her excitement from showing.

'There's someone to see you in our guest office,' she said excitedly. 'It's a girl. She looks like a film star.' Cindy had been the most welcoming of all the staff at the hotel. When she spoke slowly, her speech was elocution-lesson perfect, but when she got excited, the Norfolk accent came through. This endeared her to Steve and Emily, who both had accents just waiting to be used at appropriate moments. Emily's was North London and Steve's pure Norfolk.

'We don't get to meet many film stars, Cindy,' said Steve. 'Did she give you a name?'

'No, I didn't like to ask. It might have sounded nosey. Was that wrong?'

'No that's fine Cindy,' said Emily. 'Give us our key now, and we will go and see who it is. The office is over there isn't it?' She pointed to the corridor.

They had both guessed who it might be but hoped it wasn't her because the plans had been made and most could not be changed. They collected Lizzie from the office and took her up by the back stairs to their room, to avoid taking her through the foyer again.

They could immediately tell that something was wrong, but filled the time walking upstairs with small talk. Once in the room, Lizzie sat down and took her dark glasses off. One eye had gone completely black and blue, there were some bruises on both cheeks, and a small cut on her forehead, which she said must have been from one of the rings he was wearing.

She told them what had happened. How she had triggered it off with the remark about Barnack's murder. She kept apologising for what she had done, after all, they were doing for her.

Emily said she was not to blame at all. In that state of mind, he could have picked on anything as an excuse for hitting her. Steve agreed and said the only thing that had changed was the need to keep her safe for a couple of extra days.

'Where have you parked your car?' Steve asked.

'I left it on the Runton Road, just past the fish and chip shop. It's not far from here.' Lizzie said. She seemed to be relaxing a little now that Steve was beginning to work out what they should do next.

'I'll take it and find somewhere to hide it and then rent one that you and Will can use. Do you think you would be safe at your cottage in Salthouse, with a different car parked outside and without Will's white van giving the game away?'

'Yes, Will and you two are the only people who have been there, and I am sure no one else knows about it. I bought it myself by saving some of the money Micky gave me and putting it together with some money my father gave me when I was eighteen. Micky was very generous in the first couple of years we were together, and I never told him about the money from my father. Saving money was something I had been brought up with at home, and the money Micky gave me was super generous because he was trying to buy my love and loyalty.

I bought the cottage with cash, straight from the owner and he was moving to Australia, to be near his daughter.

'Yes, that sounds safe enough, it's just if people nearby gossip,' he said. 'You know what it is like in a small place like that. Stay indoors as much as possible, but keep your eyes open to anything suspicious happening outside.'

'What about your clothes and things?' Emily asked.

'Oh yes, they are in a case in the boot of my car.'

'I'll transfer it to the rental car,' Steve said. 'I'd better get going now. You stay here with Lizzie. And then you can find a way to contact Will.' Steve gave Emily a quick kiss and then was on his way.

'Do you have any way to contact Will when he gets back with the catch?' Emily asked.

'For times when we plan to meet, we go to a place near the pier. If it is just a casual meeting, which usually means that I need to see Will because I am feeling low, I park my car at the top of the Gangway and wait for him to see me. When he finishes work, he comes to me in the car. He keeps some clothes at my cottage.'

'Okay, when is he due back?'

Lizzie checked her watch. 'They will be back already; I would have been going down to the Gangway about now.'

'Right, I'll go down and find him and tell him what the plans are. I'll bring him back and sneak him in through the back door and stairs. Then we'll wait for Steve to return.'

She put on the anorak which was always a useful item of clothing to have, simply because it had a large hood that covered her head and most of her face. She pulled the hood up and walked out onto the parking area in front of the hotel. She quickly scanned the people standing or sitting outside. Everything seemed normal, except for the two men, talking together near the car park entrance.

The man facing her turned away far too quickly, and the other one couldn't resist a quick look. Okay, they were amateurs, and it wouldn't be any problem to lose them. But Emily wanted to know who they were and, more importantly, who they were looking for.

She walked down the sloping, zig-zag path to the promenade, making sure that they didn't lose her. And then, coming up to where the crab boats were, she stopped and watched the men putting the crabs into containers.

Will spotted Emily, and at once his face showed concern. Emily smiled and gave him a little wave to reassure him that everything was okay. He waved and went back to his work. One of the other fishermen said something, and they all laughed. Will looked at Emily and shrugged his shoulders.

Emily turned and saw the two men skulking near the promenade wall. Good, they were still there. After about ten minutes more, Will left his boat and came walking over to Emily.

'It's nothing to worry about,' Emily said to him. 'In fact, I think it's good news. Lizzie has walked out on Micky because he started to get violent and slap her about.'

'Is she okay now?' Will asked.

'Apart from a few bruises, she is all right, but he seems to be a man on the brink, lashing out at anyone. She is safe in our hotel room, and Steve has gone to hide her car and then rent another one for her.

'Would you be able to get a couple of days off?' Emily asked.

'Yes, it's all fixed, I could see that this was coming sometime this week and the blokes have said they will cover for me.'

'That's good. Can you get away now?'

'Yes, I'm ready.'

'Just before we go, can you see the men behind me, one quite tall and thin and the other a stocky little guy?'

'Yes, I see them,' said Will.

'Do you know them? They have followed me from the hotel, very badly I might say, but I would love to know who they're working for.'

'I've seen them in the pub a few times, so they must be locals, but I don't know them. Let's go and ask them why they are following you,' he said.

'I was hoping you would say that,' Emily said with a smile.

They turned and walked straight towards the men who hesitated for a second or two, and then turned and hurried away.

'Now why did they do that?' said Emily, who had been looking forward to the confrontation.

'Could be because I've got about twenty mates working on the boats behind us. And crab fishermen look out for each other. I think those two, whoever they are, were very wise on this occasion.'

They got back to the hotel, and Emily led Will in through to the back stairs. Lizzie ran to Will and clung tightly to him, crying with happiness that she was with him again. Emily looked out of the window, and Lizzie told Will the story of what had happened and how she decided that she had to get away from Micky.

It was another hour before Steve returned and there was a difficult moment when there was a knock at the door, and the maid wanted to turn down the bed covers. Emily opened the door a few inches and said that her husband was tired and was taking a nap.

Lizzie said, 'I didn't know that you and Steve were married?'

'We are not, but as you can see this is a very traditional hotel, so rather than cause any embarrassment, I carry a ring around with me. I wouldn't bother with it in London, but I didn't want to take the risk here, particularly as we were trying to keep a low profile.'

'Do you plan to get married?' Lizzie asked.

'Yes,' said Emily. 'But every time we start to make arrangements, a new assignment comes along and off we go. We'll manage it some time, but when you freelance, as we do, you have to take the work when it comes.'

Steve had also used the back stairs and said that everything was ready for them to go. The car was parked where Lizzie had left hers, and her case was in the boot. Emily and Steve walked down with Lizzie and Will and watched them walking away towards the car. Emily had told Steve about the men who had followed her, so they walked slowly down the street behind Lizzie and Will to make certain that nobody had followed them.

CHAPTER 29

Micky drove through the town to see Shay and tell him that Lizzie had gone. Micky walked around the house and found Shay, digging in his garden.

'Bloody hell Shay, are you still pissing about with that.'

'I've got to like it. Never thought I would, but it's very relaxing, and I'm learning a lot about how to grow vegetables.'

'I can think of better ways to relax,' said Micky. 'Put that fucking fork down and let's talk indoors. We've got problems'

'What, with those two journalists I told you about?'

'Yes them,

and Lizzie's fucked off.' He sat down on a kitchen chair as if he was exhausted.

'What, left you, or just gone off in a strop?'

'Could be either, but I reckon she thinks it's for good. The trouble is,' Micky continued, 'she knows how to press my buttons. She said that she knew I was mixed up in Barnack's murder and that set me off. I slapped her around a bit, nothing really bad, but I'd never lifted a finger to her before. We'd had a few shouting matches, but nothing really serious.'

Shay shook his head. 'Girls of today don't like that sort of thing. When my mammy was alive, back in Ireland, it was a regular occurrence in our house, and I never heard her complain. But you can't do that sort of thing these days.'

'What do you think I should do?'

'We could go looking for her, but I think that could just draw attention to the situation.'

'You think so?'

'Yes, I do. Let her go if she wants to. She is not going to kick up a fuss. She's too involved with all this. She's been living with you for god knows how many years, so she's got as much to lose as us?'

'Okay, we'll leave it at that then?'

Micky stood up to leave. He now had proof of what he suspected all along. Shay is fucking Lizzie. That is why he doesn't want to look for her. He already knows where she is. The bastard. And Shay had tried to tell him that she was having an affair with a fucking crab fisherman. A likely bloody story. No wonder they used to ignore each other when he was around. Okay, if Shay wants to play it that way, Micky Naylor is ready for him. He had already lined up a bunch of local blokes to go and search for Lizzie. Good job he hadn't told Shay. He was going to, but a gut feeling told him to hold back. Well, once they have dealt with Lizzie, they can take care of Shay.

Then another thought entered his head. This mysterious fucker who left the message with Lizzie. Shay was in the Army, and this other cunt sounds as though he was as well. Shay must have recruited him to help drive me out of the business. Well, it will take a lot more than a couple of Army has-beens to get rid of Micky Naylor. Bring it on.

He drove back to the house on Cliff Drive and let himself in. It was quiet, and Lizzie had not returned. From the bravado of a few minutes ago, Micky was beginning to doubt himself again. He almost expected Lizzie to be back. Never mind, these local lads know what they are doing. They will soon have her under control.

CHAPTER 30

The next day Will woke with the sun streaming through the bedroom window. He and Lizzie had decided to sleep in the back bedroom and hide the car on the lawn at the back of the cottage. To anyone passing it would look as though there was no one there. It was an additional safety measure that Will decided would make Lizzie even safer.

As promised, Will called the hotel and asked to speak to Steve. He was put through immediately.

'Hello Steve, it's me,' he said. 'Calling in as promised.'

'Are you both okay?'

'Yes, all seems quiet here. We are keeping away from the front windows, but I can see pretty well in both directions, and there seems to be no one about.'

'I called my editor last night, and he said that he would call the Security people.'

'That's great,' said Will. 'Lizzie is very shaken still, but she is sleeping, so she should feel a little better when she wakes.'

'Yes, I am sure she will,' said Steve. 'Take care, and I will call you when I have any more news.'

'Thanks, mate. You and Emily take care too, you are nearest the trouble now.'

Will went to the cupboard to make a cup of coffee while he waited for Lizzie to wake. The cupboard was empty. Then he remembered that Lizzie hated leaving anything edible because of the mice and rats that hung around in the old farm buildings at the bottom of the garden. What the cottage needed was permanent residents, with a nice cat or dog to keep scavengers out. And he knew just the people to make it the perfect home.

He sat down at the kitchen table and wrote a short note for Lizzie.

'Just gone to the shop down the road. Keep away from front windows. I am going through the yard at the back, and across the field so I'm not seen. Love you, Will.'

He stepped out into the back garden. The sun was doing its best to warm a chill breeze, but the little village of Salthouse looked magical in this light. Will locked the door behind him and made his way down the garden. He loved early mornings when the air was cold and fresh. It made you feel alive and ready for anything.

The farmyard was no longer in use, but a few hens were making their way through the long grass and weeds, picking up bits and pieces as they went. They must belong to one of the other cottages, thought Will as he stepped over the stone wall that marked where the yard stopped, and the field started. The wall had toppled over onto its side, so it was an easy stride over it.

His walk through the field was only about 50 yards before he came to the five-bar gate, climbed over it and headed along the track to the road. Having a quick look around, but seeing no one, he walked the few yards to the small shop.

He had never been in the shop before, so the shopkeeper would not know him. He bought bread, milk, jam, butter, ham, cheese, coffee, tea and biscuits. He thought that would keep them going until help arrived. As he stepped outside the shop, the bus from Cromer had stopped to let a couple of people off. The heavy clothes they were wearing, along with the binoculars and cameras that hung from their necks, told him they were bird watchers. It was almost a uniform in these parts.

He retraced his steps back to the house and came up to the back door. Will had taken the key out of his pocket and put it in the door before he saw a small square in the kitchen door window had been broken. For a second, his brain wouldn't believe what his eyes were seeing. Then reality and panic kicked-in in equal measure. He dashed into the kitchen. The note he had left was still on the table. Maybe he had disturbed them, and Lizzie was sleeping soundly upstairs. He clawed his way up the stairs, stumbling on his knees and then staggering into the bedroom. Lizzie had gone.

CHAPTER 31

Lizzie was having a dream. She was drinking a glass of wine, sitting in a red room. The curtains were red, the carpet was red, and her wine was red. It suddenly slipped from her hand and fell onto the thickly piled carpet, but instead of bouncing on the carpet, it smashed into tiny slivers of glass, small slithers scattering over the floor.

She tried to stand, but something was preventing her from moving. She grasped at the red tablecloth in front of her and pulled it towards her. No matter how much she pulled, the tablecloth came towards her until it was nearly covering her. Then she felt it being tugged away from her, but she couldn't see who was pulling it.

Then she saw it was two men, standing either side of the chair. She began to wake, and the chair became the bed, and the two men were real. She looked frantically around her. Where was Will? She called his name. Then she screamed his name.

'Shut the fuck up, you fucking stuck-up slut. You'll wake the neighbours'

'What have you done to Will?' she cried. She looked around and thought she saw him, but soon realised there was another man in the room. She kicked and screamed and twisted her body and managed to pull one arm free. She flung herself at the man who was still holding her and managed to scratch his face. The third man joined the struggle and managed to get hold of her arm. They dragged her out the bed, and she flopped on the floor and lay there sobbing.

The short baby doll nightdress was fashionable but impractical in this situation. The matching panties had slid a short way down her thighs and were attracting the close attention of the man who had let her arm go. He leant forward to touch her when the man who she had scratched shouted. 'Bert, what the fuck are you doing?'

'I was just having a quick feel. She is sexy. Wow, just look at that,' said Bert.

'Jesus bloody Christ, this is Micky's wife. We are supposed to be taking her back to him, not groping her. Well, if she tells him I'm going to say it was you and you alone that did it. He will go ape-shit, and we're not taking any of the blame, are we Alf?'

'No, we're bloody not.'

'Pull 'em up,' he said in a harsh whisper to Lizzie, as if it was her fault.

She did as much as she could, but they roughly picked her up and began to carry her down the stairs. Bert was allocated an arm to carry, as was Alf. The man she had scratched, had his huge hands wrapped around her ankles. Lizzie soon found out that he was Ron, and he was in charge.

A dilapidated old van was backed right up to the back door. Lizzie was bundled in through the back doors and laid down on an old piece of tarpaulin, with a dirty old sack placed in the middle of it. If it was meant to add to her comfort, it failed miserably. The scratchy surface of the sacking felt like sandpaper on Lizzie's bare skin.

But she was not complaining or fighting anymore. She had taken all the humiliation and fear that she could handle. She lay in the back of the rickety old van and tried to work out what had gone wrong. Where was Will? Had they hurt him?

Ron was driving the van. He pulled out onto the road and accelerated as fast as he could towards Cromer. To her relief, Bert the groper was in the passenger seat, and Alf sat on an old apple box just behind Ron. Lizzie lay at an angle across the back of the van, that rattled along the road at a speed it was not designed for. There was a strong smell of exhaust fumes, where Lizzie lay.

Alf was trying not to look at Lizzie, but his eyes kept being drawn back to her. Lizzie propped herself up on one elbow and looked Alf in the eyes. She wanted him to recognise that she was a real human being and not just something to lust after. At least Ron had had the decency to insist that Bert sat up front with him.

'What happened to Will?' she asked. 'Have you hurt him?'

Alf gave a little laugh. 'No, we didn't have to. He went shopping at the wrong time. We parked down the road, and Ron and me came to see how we could get you. We had been watching the place for about half-an-hour when your boyfriend comes out and into the old farmyard, where I was hiding. He went across the field and then turned down the track. He could have only been going to the shop. I legged it back to the cottage, Ron signalled for Alf to bring the van and within ten minutes, you were in it, and here we are on our way. Simple as that. We're a good team.'

All three of them were enjoying their moments of glory. Ron was chuckling away as Alf told the story. He never thought it would go as well as this. Even Bert was cheering up after the telling-off he had received from Ron. Bert turned in his seat and looked at Lizzie.

'Yes, she's a real beauty alright,' he said, leering at Lizzie.

'Leave it out, Bert. We are not bloody animals. Just behave yourself.'

Bert reluctantly turned back to look out of the front windscreen. 'I can't see any reason why we shouldn't have a bit of fun with her.'

'I'm saying this for your own good. Micky would cut your bollocks off if you did anything to her. She's his wife.'

'I suppose so,' grumbled Bert.

For once, Lizzie was pleased that Micky's reputation was saving her from even more ill-treatment than she had received already. But she also knew that Ron's reasoning was a long way from reality. Micky was going to deal with her when they took her back, and unless Will, Steve and Emily could track them down, she was in real trouble.

They drove for about half-an-hour before the van slowed and Ron turned off the road. They bounced along a small track and then turned into what seemed to be a field. Bert then jumped out of the van, while Ron waited with the engine running.

She heard banging and scraping noises and then the van was driven slowly forward, and everything seemed to go dark. Lizzie could hardly see anything inside the van. She instinctively drew her legs up and wrapped her arms around them in a defensive ball.

The back doors opened, and Ron was standing there looking down at Lizzie. She looked passed him and saw that the van was now inside a large barn. Bert was closing two big doors, which he did by kicking them along, as they scraped over the uneven ground. Lizzie suddenly felt sick, although she couldn't decide if it was the sight of Bert or the exhaust fumes that made her feel unwell. She was cold in the scanty night clothes that she had on and she began to shiver.

'Come on,' said Ron. 'You're getting cold. You can't walk across this floor; it's covered in broken glass and rusty nails. I'll carry you, and then we'll find something to keep you warm.'

The high-octane frenzy of the abduction had gone now, and Ron and Alf had turned back into less threatening people. Lizzie was calm, but she still didn't trust Bert.

'Ron lifted her out of the van with ease and carried her quickly over to a caravan, which was parked in the middle of the large, dilapidated barn. It was without a roof at one end and had partially collapsed at one corner. In contrast, the caravan looked comparatively new and clean.

Alf held the door open, and Ron carried her into the caravan and sat her down on a long seat that ran around one end. There was a large window that gave a panoramic view of the barn.

'I'll go and get something to keep you warm,' Ron said. He came back with a large double blanket that Lizzie wrapped around herself.

Lizzie thanked him and then said, 'You know Micky is going to kill me, don't you?'

'Look,' said Ron, appearing a little agitated. 'We are getting paid to find you and take you back to him. That's all. Whatever else is going on between you and him, is your business.'

'So, you don't care if he's going to kill me?' she asked.

'I'm sure he won't. He seemed very distressed when I spoke to him. We will take you back to Micky, and I am sure you can work something out together. I am going to send Bert out to get us some breakfast now, and I don't want to hear another word about it.'

CHAPTER 32

Will was beside himself with grief and guilt. It felt as if his whole world was collapsing. How stupid was he, to go and leave her like that? He thought she was safe here. He wanted to surprise her with a nice breakfast and show her how good life could be with him. He wanted her to know how much he cared about her. Instead, he had put her in great danger, with that crazy idiot of a husband, likely to do anything to her. He was almost crying, but he knew he had to get himself under control if he was going to find her.

He looked at his watch. Would Steve and Emily still be in the Hotel? He hoped so.

He dialled the number and waited what seemed like an eternity for someone to answer. A male voice said. 'Hotel de Paris, how may I help you.'

'Could you put me through to Mr and Mrs Moon's room please.' He wanted to shout, 'and get a bloody move on', but he had to remain calm.

Steve answered almost at once.

'It's Will. They have taken Lizzie.'

There was silence on the line for a second or two as Steve's brain almost rejected the possibility of what he had just heard.

'She's been taken. How?'

'It was all my fault said Will,' and then proceeded to tell him about going to the village shop, because they had forgotten to get anything in last night, and how he returned to find the broken window pane and Lizzie gone.

'It's not your fault; you had to get things in. They must have just been waiting for a chance, and it happened to come along, without them having to use any strong-arm stuff. They sound like a professional crew to pull off a smooth operation like that. Put blaming yourself out of your mind. Come over to us now, and we will work out a way to get her back.'

'Thanks, Steve, I'm on my way.'

Will parked the car at the front of the hotel and went to the reception desk. Cindy was on duty, and she directed Will to the breakfast room where Steve and Emily were waiting for him. He walked over to them looking like a broken man and slumped down into a chair. He accepted the offer of a cup of coffee but was too distraught to eat anything.

'I don't know where to start,' said Will gloomily.

'Well, what about those two characters who were following me yesterday. You said that you had seen them in a pub. Which pub?'

'I can't remember, but it must have been one of those close by, around Jetty street, High Street or New Street. I only go to other pubs when I'm with Lizzie,' he said miserably.

'Okay,' said Emily, 'as soon as they open we go in all of them and ask if they know who they were. Why would they be following me if it wasn't something to do with Lizzie and Micky?'

Steve nodded, 'It must be something to do with it. Find them, and we might find Lizzie. Did they look like pros to you?' Steve asked Emily.

'No, far from it. They were just blundering along, making no effort to disguise what they were doing.'

'It sounds to me that you were just unlucky Will. They must have been waiting around for something to happen, and it did. I can't imagine that they had been waiting all night. These things happen, and nobody is to blame. Let's do what Emily suggests and get out there and find who these men are.'

'In the meantime,' said Will, I will go and ask the blokes I work with. They go to the same pubs as I do, so they might know something about them. It will be best if I ask them on my own. It takes them a while to get used to strangers.'

'Okay, and we will see if we can find Eric and ask him if he knows them,' Steve said.

CHAPTER 33

Steve had been unable to reach Eric. He was working on a new house in North Walsham. So, Steve and Emily sat in a small café near the pier entrance and waited for Will to come back and report on what he had found out about the two men that had followed Emily.

'Thinking back,' Emily said, 'they were waiting for me at the hotel and followed me to the crab boats. Maybe it wasn't me they were looking for, it must have been Lizzie. I think they knew that she might contact us and by now it must be common knowledge where we are staying. When I led them to Will, it proved they were on the right track, but it spooked them when we walked straight towards them, so they certainly didn't want any conversation. I think they were hoping to get lucky and just to grab her. There was probably a third man in a car or van, waiting in the back streets to abduct Lizzie and there is no prize for guessing who was paying them.'

'Yes, but how did they know about Lizzie's cottage at Salthouse?' said Steve. 'She said she had taken precautions to hide its ownership.'

'It must have been when Will and I scared them off. I bet they just walked around the corner and waited until she came out. Of course,' said Emily. 'They already knew she was there. They had seen her go in and probably weren't ready to make the snatch. They must have seen us walking along behind checking that no one was watching. They would have spotted where her car was parked and just followed them to the cottage. Then it was a case of playing the waiting game until Will wasn't around.'

'Yes, that all fits. Well let's hope that Will can find us some leads to follow, we need to find her before they deliver her to Micky. I think he has decided that she knows too much to let her go. When she walked out, he dare not let his boss in Europe know that she had gone.'

'I don't think we should tell Will about what we think until we have some evidence. He looks miserable enough as it is and blames himself and we need someone who still has hope,' said Steve.

CHAPTER 34

Lizzie still felt like a mess, but she was a little happier than before. Ron had managed to find a freshly washed shirt and lent it to Lizzie to cover herself more effectively than the baby dolls did. She still kept them on but covered everything underneath with the shirt. Ron was at least six-foot-tall and thin, so the shirt covered her quite well, even though there were a few buttons missing and it smelt musty.

She wasn't allowed shoes so that there was no way she could make a dash for freedom across the mud floor, which was covered in broken glass and rusty nails. Ron had made a couple of trips to the nearest telephone kiosk to negotiate terms for Lizzie's return to Micky, but it appeared that having agreed on a price with him, Ron now thought that Lizzie's value was considerably higher than Micky's offer.

The result seems to be a standoff, with Micky refusing to pay a penny more and Ron determined to get a much better deal now he had seen the quality of the merchandise. Lizzie looked on this as being a far better situation than before. It didn't matter to her that they were negotiating her value as if she was a prize bull.

It was Ron's reasoning that fascinated Lizzie. Because she was prettier than expected, she must be worth more. So, if she had some nice clothes to put on and could get her hair washed and put on some makeup, she could easily raise the asking price. She was going to mention it to Ron, but she knew he didn't really like her and was only being decent to her because of Micky. Well, unfortunately for Ron, if there was one thing that could really annoy Micky, it was someone trying to put one over on him when making a deal. In Micky's mind, he was the hustler supreme. Ron was playing with fire, but let him find out.

She could move around in the caravan and was in far less danger here than she would have been with Micky. She had even cleaned the place up and offered to make a meal for everyone.

The store cupboard was, however, somewhat limited, comprising mainly of tins of beef stew, without labels, tins of baked beans and a sack of potatoes, many of which were going mouldy. But she did her best with it, and they all sat down around the small table and ate as if they were some dysfunctional family. Ron spoke continually about what sort of van he was going to buy with the money they got for Lizzie's return. Alf was looking forward to spending a few days with his small son in Great Yarmouth. He was apparently separated from his wife. Lizzie listened with great interest and commented when necessary, thinking that she might eventually talk them into letting her go. Bert just sat and looked at Lizzie.

Ron went off in the afternoon for another attempt at negotiating a better deal. He came back half-an-hour later fuming about Micky's pig headedness. Lizzie didn't know whether to warn him about Micky and what sort of a man he was, but she didn't think that Ron would believe her. If he had known what Micky was capable of, and if he was an even slightly intelligent man, he would take her straight to the house on Cliff Drive and give Micky a couple of hundred pounds for letting him do the job. But now, it was all too late. Ron would be very fortunate to survive even a few more days.

When Ron got Lizzie on her own, he asked her quietly if her other bloke might be more generous if he returned her untouched. Lizzie assured Ron that he would be very generous. Ron seemed to cheer up at that news and said that if Micky didn't change his mind soon, he would make a deal with her boyfriend. That night Lizzie went to sleep on the hard cushions of the long seat in the caravan feeling excited that by tomorrow this could all be over. Steve and Emily would know how to handle this sort of situation.

CHAPTER 35

Joe had just discovered that the modest little house almost opposite Micky's flashy Villa, was a holiday home. Its owners were apparently enjoying themselves on the Riviera at the moment. He had quickly let himself in. The Army had trained him well on picking locks, so he was soon making himself comfortable in the upstairs bedroom that looked straight down onto Micky's driveway and front door. He quickly went to the shop in the town and bought some essential supplies, before returning to the house. His sleeping bag and other bits and pieces were already in the kitchen downstairs.

Joe felt that this was a great breakthrough in his mission. And what he was doing was a mission; for nearly twenty-years it had been slowly gnawing at his patience and resolve. It threatened to explode into rash thinking and poor planning, which would have been against everything that he had learnt throughout his career in the Army. Clear thinking, good planning and above all, good intelligence, these were the things that got the job done and kept you alive.

Now that he had completed his duties for Queen and Country, he would be able to look after the unfinished family business.

But it had been difficult, coming here, to this unfamiliar part of the UK and suddenly dealing with civilians. It is so different from the Army that it was almost like landing on another planet. Joe knew that his many solo missions had turned him into a bit of a recluse and even when he worked in a small team, the other guys were just as introverted as he was.

Added to this, he was a Londoner, with all the impatient traits that brought. These Norfolk people were nice and friendly, but they were not going to hurry themselves. Ask them a straight question, and it would take them ten minutes to get to the point. Here, the conversation was for fun, and the taller the story, the more they enjoyed it. They also liked to have a bit of fun with strangers, pretending they didn't understand when you knew very well they did.

Joe also knew, that even when he was trying to be nice and friendly, he did scare people. This came from the situations he had faced many times in the Army when talking to civilians in dangerous situations. A quick answer could be the difference between life and death.

But, a good soldier should be able to work anywhere. His mission was to avenge his brother's death, and it should not bother him how difficult things had been.

Young Barry, or 'Nipper', as he was known, was three years younger than Joe. He was called Nipper, not only because he was small, but also because he was always doing something, and it was usually something that would get him into trouble. In the family home in South London, Nipper was always just going to or coming back from somewhere. And, within minutes, he was gone again. He was also not a great judge of friends. He always chose the stupid, but very active boys, who would lead him and themselves into trouble, without even realising there was anything wrong.

It meant a tough time for his parents, so Joe, at the age of eleven, decided to ditch his friends and take the responsibility of keeping Barry on the straight and narrow. Joe was a serious boy and probably not a lot of fun to be with, especially if you were one of his eleven-year-old friends. But Barry had always loved to go out with big brother Joe. Joe was adventurous, but always very sensible. It was a risk-free adventure, and Nipper seemed to enjoy the greater freedom that came with going around with Joe.

Their mother would always be told where they were going and what time they were coming home. Other boys never tried to bully Nipper when he was with Joe because they were scared to death of him. He was a well-built young boy for an eleven-year-old, and he could have passed for fifteen. But he also carried a quiet menace in his demeanour. As a result, word got out not to pick a fight with Joe. And he never picked a fight with anyone; unnecessary violence was not in Joe's nature.

Their dad was seldom at home, because he was in the Army, as had his father before him. Joe had obviously inherited the calmness and reliability that Army people need, and now he had stepped up to take his father's role while he was away. His dad was always very proud of him when he came home on leave, and the three of them used to go on adventures together.

By the time the second world war came along, their dad had retired and started a small taxi business. The Army was always going to be Joe's career, and at the age of seventeen he signed up, and after two months the war broke out. Joe's talent was soon recognised, and he was transferred to special services.

Three years later Barry was called up and, with a bit of help from dad, managed to get into the transport division of the Royal Engineers. Joe and his dad both recognised that Nipper's impetuous nature would not go down well in the fighting services and hoped that transport could keep him out of harm's way.

But, to their surprise, Nipper seem to be getting on well. He would write to them from time to time and as the war began to be won, his letters got more frequent and more confident. They received a letter, which was full of excitement telling them how, he and his mate Micky, had just driven a load of supplies into the newly captured Berlin.

Then, the letters became less frequent, but it still sounded as though Barry was having a great time with his mate Micky. Then suddenly, the letters stopped. No one in the family worried particularly about it. This was just like the Nipper they knew only too well. No news would mean that he was enjoying himself so much, that there was no time to write letters to the family.

These family assumptions were proved completely wrong when a letter came from his Commanding Officer, saying that Barry had committed suicide while remanded in an Army prison on charges of theft and profiteering. Joe later found out that his mate Micky had worked out a scheme where they delivered three-quarters of the supplies they were carrying to their proper destination, and then diverted the remaining quarter to the black market. As they hadn't even paid for the goods, they were making huge profits.

The city of Berlin was virtually destroyed, but awash with money. The Russian troops, who hadn't been paid for three months because of lack of funds, now had their hands on plenty of cash; their troops were given full back pay in the form of coupons, which could only be used in Berlin and would have no value once they were back in Russia. What they couldn't spend on prostitutes, they spent on other luxury goods. And almost anything was a luxury in war-torn Russia.

But it wasn't just the Russians. It was commonplace in post-war Berlin. Everyone seemed to have a scam going, the Americans, the British, the Russians, and everyone else.

It went on for about a year before the Military, who was supposed to be running the City, decided to clamp down and bring in some law and order. The British asked for teams of civilian police to be brought in, as their skills were very different from those of Military Police.

They offered a full pardon to anyone involved in the fraud, providing they named all others who were part of the scam. Micky saw his opportunity, and without telling Nipper, stepped up and admitted his role in the scam. According to him, however, he could only give back a small amount of the profits. He claimed that the nasty Russians had got wind of his decision to own up to his misdoings and a gang of them had given him a heavy beating until he told them where his and Nipper's stash was hidden.

Micky was immediately discharged from the Army but remarkably, was able to set up a legitimate wholesale business as soon as he got home to London; an amazing achievement on Army wages.

As a result of Micky naming him, Nipper was arrested and told he would face charges of theft and profiteering, which would result in a prison sentence and dishonourable discharge from the Army.

In the letter he sent just before he killed himself, saying how sorry he was for what he had done, he said the prison sentence would have been hard, but it was deserved. What he couldn't take was the shame he had brought to his family and their proud Army record. He was found hanged in his cell just a week before Micky started his wholesale business, which Joe was happy to hear failed after six months.

Most of the things that he now knew, he only discovered after his Army career came to an end a few weeks ago. The big war was over, but it was changing attitudes and boundaries throughout the world. There were small wars springing up in Asia, Africa, South America and even Europe. His skills were those of the secret soldier who went to war without anyone knowing and came back again without anyone noticing. That was what Joe called a mission accomplished. Nothing less would do.

When he first knew about Micky and what he had done to Barry, he tried to put it behind him, but it always came back. Even laying in the Sahara Desert, in his little tent, so tired, hungry and cold that he could hardly remember what mission he was on, it would be there, eating away at him. He would make himself feel better by imagining what he would do to Micky. It was always at some time in the future. Until, last year, when he nearly failed the yearly medical.

Then he suddenly thought, why put it off any longer? He would have one more year and then go and work for a private security company. That is where the big money is these days. And before he had to go off to Timbuctoo or wherever, he would find Micky Naylor and put the record straight.

That was how he found himself sitting in a borrowed bedroom, looking down at Micky's smart house, complete with swimming pool. It had taken him longer than he had hoped to get it organised to his standards, but he was ready now, and he would take the opportunity as soon as he could. He had been here since lunchtime and had seen no sign of Micky or his wife. From what he had heard from the locals, their marriage seemed to be running very close to the rocks. His visit to the house the other evening confirmed that she was having a fling with a young man from the town. Well good luck to her, she seemed to be much too nice for a rat like Micky. Let's hope she stays out of the way, he thought.

CHAPTER 36

Time went by exceedingly slowly in the caravan. Ron, Alf, and Bert came and went, but Lizzie never left. As it was parked in the barn, it was quite difficult to tell night from day.

Lizzie was still wearing her make-do outfit of baby doll pyjamas and Ron's shirt, and she was feeling increasingly optimistic that she would not be returned to Micky, with all the dangers that might hold for her.

Ron was getting very stressed, however, because things were not turning out as planned. He had obviously seen easy money on the horizon when Micky approached him in the pub to find Lizzie and bring her back to him. But things had not gone to plan, and Ron's demand for more money must have sent Micky into one of his rages. He never liked not getting his way, and someone is trying to put one over on him was more than he would be able to stand. He was the man that could drive a hard bargain, not some local upstart like Ron.

The thing that worried Lizzie most was Micky's reaction to the telephone call from Ron. If Micky still refused to deal, she would encourage Ron to call Will. That would at least tell Will that she was still alive.

But when the subject of paying a ransom came up, and Ron told Will what he wanted, Will would inevitably say that he did not have that sort of money. He wouldn't be able to stop himself. It's how Will was, honest. That's what she loved about him, after all the lies and deception she had from Micky; Will had restored her faith in human nature.

She hoped that Emily and Steve were on hand to advise Will. They would almost certainly know what to do.

In the meantime, she had to wait and hope. She could see that Ron was getting desperate and wondered how Alf and Bert would take the news that Micky had turned his back on the deal. Alf, she thought, would go along with anything Ron said, but Bert she did not trust. He was morose since the telling off by Ron, but if Ron's deal didn't come off, she hated to think what would happen.

If the two of them decided to walk away from this, they surely wouldn't leave her with Bert. He had been keeping his distance, but that could all change quickly, and she certainly didn't want the fat, slimy sod climbing all over her.

Ron had been away, making another effort to speak to Micky. As she watched him trudging back across the mud floor, Alf and Bert came to see if he looked cheerful or not. He looked grim, which, although Lizzie didn't say anything, she was secretly pleased. Alf turned away to watch Ron come into the caravan, but Bert moved closer to her and placed a hand on her bare leg and moved it up under the shirt to her thigh. He moved his face until it touched her ear.

'Just you wait. If Ron decides to cut his losses and run, we can have some fun.' Bert whispered, his foul breath almost making her sick. She tried to push him away, but he was too heavy. He was in no hurry to get off her. Obviously, Ron didn't scare him anymore. Bert let his hand slip round to her inner thighs and then push himself off her as Ron looked across at them. He didn't say anything to Bert.

'The fucking line's dead now. I don't know what is going on. I'll leave it until tomorrow and then call your other bloke,' he said to Lizzie, seemingly not noticing Bert had sat down beside her. Bert reached around Lizzie's back and brought his hand round and felt her left breast. She tried to pull away from him, but he persisted.

'Leave it out Bert, will you. We have got other things to worry about.' Ron said in a matter of fact way.

CHAPTER 37

Back at his newly found vantage point, Joe was now certain that Micky's wife was not there. He had thought about leaving it a day or two to familiarise himself with Micky's routine. However, experience had taught him, that when everything seems to be right, it usually is right and waiting for it to be perfect is a lost opportunity.

Over the years Joe trained himself to be able to concentrate on the target while thinking about other things. In many cases the other things that he thought about was the very thing that was happening now. Meeting Micky Naylor, telling him that he was Nipper's brother, and what he was going to do. He didn't underestimate Micky, but one thing he had learnt in life was that the biggest bullies are also the biggest cowards. Micky wouldn't go quietly, but he would go.

It was dark now, and the street lighting had been on for at least an hour. A car stopped and parked down the road. This was a popular place to park in the summertime. It was close to the front, and it was free, with no time limits. Like most small towns, Cromer was not a place to come to for the nightlife. So why had this car stopped there? Could be just checking where they were on a map? Could be a couple of young people having a kiss and cuddle.

Then, two men in dark clothing stepped out of the car and began to walk up the hill towards the houses. They were carrying a holdall bag, and their body language suggested that they were relaxed. They were looking around as if they were not very familiar with the street, but their pace was steady and sure as if they knew where they were going.

To Joe's surprise, they turned into Micky's driveway and walked up to the front door. A light in the hallway was switched on, and the door opened immediately. They went in, and after a few moments the hall light went off. But nothing more happened. Joe thought he might have heard a muffled shout, but it could have just been his imagination or from another house in the street.

He saw no other sign of life from the house and sat impatiently waiting for the two visitors to go. He suddenly decided that it would be a good idea to get the car registration number, while the two men were still inside. He quickly pulled on his black windcheater and went briskly down the stairs. Outside it was quite cold. He kept close to the hedges which cast a black shadow on the pavement and made him more difficult to see. Outside he could hear no sound, except for the call of a lone wood pigeon, coming from the woods at the end of the road.

That was where Joe had tried to live rough for a few days. It didn't work. He had done it many times, for weeks on end. But there is a big difference between a Malaysian jungle and a small wood in Cromer. You don't get dozens of dog walkers, courting couples and adventurous kids running around in the jungle. For the rest of his time, he found a little one-room B&B run by an old lady, who treated him like a son. He asked her not to tell anyone that he was staying with her, and she was true to her word. When he found this place, he paid her double what she was asking as a thank you keeping the secret. He wondered what she would say after people start searching for Nosey Joe, as the locals like to call him. It will all start happening when the body of Micky is found. Joe didn't care what came out then. He would be long gone from the UK.

He memorised the number plate and headed back towards his vantage point. Joe resisted the temptation to go and see what was happening. It was probably two of Micky's team of heavies coming to discuss work. They obviously had to keep a low profile in a small town like this, hence the late meeting time when everyone was going to bed. As he passed through the kitchen, he grabbed some bread, cheese and a bottle of beer. He settled down to watch.

It was well after midnight before he saw the two men again. And, strangely, they appeared from a narrow alleyway that ran between Cliff Drive and the cliff walk, the pathway that led up to the Lighthouse and on to Overstrand. He had used that alleyway himself when he was looking around for security weaknesses. So, they must have let themselves out of the patio door on the other side of the house. There was a small gate leading to the pathway. He had seen the man who Micky's wife was having an affair with, slipping in through the gate on the night he went looking for Micky. He's a brave young man to go messing with Micky Naylor's wife. Joe felt bad about the way he had to handle that scene. It had surprised him, not finding Micky. He had felt sure that was him coming home, through the back gate. But it was very dark, and he had never seen Micky before.

Using the alleyway wasn't a bad idea if you wanted to reduce the risk of being seen and it was close to where they had parked the car.

Joe looked at his watch. He would not rush things. That is how mistakes are made. He would wait an hour, and Micky should be asleep by then.

That would make it easy, but it wouldn't matter if he were still awake. Joe knew he could still take him. Micky was a man who told others to kill. Joe is a man who killed because his country needed him to. He didn't choose the targets, and it wasn't for him to ask if it was fair or not. He didn't decide who lived or died, but he was willing to make one exception – Micky Naylor.

At one-o-clock in the morning, Joe decided that the time had come. He had waited and considered if he was doing the right thing. There were many arguments for and against, but each time he came back to one conclusion. Micky Naylor had been involved in many murders over the years and had always managed to evade justice. Killing him was not just about revenge for what he did to Barry. It was for all the others and at least two here in Cromer.

Joe stood up and picked up a small bag, checked inside that he had everything he needed and then walked steadily downstairs. He checked that the street was empty and then ran quietly across the road in his rubber-soled boots.

He produced a small set of tools from his pocket and within seconds was inside. He was surprised the door wasn't on a chain, but at least it saved him a few seconds. He walked silently and methodically through the downstairs, carefully checking under furniture and in cupboards.

Now for the trickier bit upstairs. The broad, open steps of the stairs were made of solid wood so that Joe could reach the top landing without a sound. It was obviously an addition to the house because as soon as he stepped onto the landing, it creaked. It was not a loud sound, more of a soft groan, but it was enough to wake a light sleeper.

He stopped, waited and listened. After a couple of minutes, he moved forward again, carefully testing each board he was about to stand on. It was slow work but necessary. There were three bedrooms. One was a smallish guest room, the next was immediately recognisable as a female's bedroom, with plenty of mirrors, a large dressing table and lots of cushions. He also noted that it had had a new lock added recently, confirmation that their marriage was heading for the rocks.

The next room had to be Micky's. Joe pulled a small pistol from his pocket, with a silencer fitted to the barrel. He would only use it if absolutely necessary. The gun was unreliable at more than five metres, but great for close quarter work. He gently opened the door and froze as the hinges gave a pained groan. It was enough to wake the whole house. The figure lying in bed did not make a move. He quickly pulled a touch from his pocket and flashed it around the room. The gun was steady in his right hand. The figure on the bed turned out to be two pillows laid casually on the bed. It wasn't intentional to fool him; it was just the way they had fallen.

Joe was puzzled. Was Micky in the house? He could have gone out of the patio doors, just as his night visitors had. Has he decided to cut and run and the two men were helping him? Micky must have so many enemies; he must have always been thinking about his own safety. He may have gone out earlier in the evening, while Joe was watching the front of the house. That would mean he was on foot because all his cars were on the driveway. It seemed very unlikely.

That thought reminded Joe that he hadn't checked the garage. But if he was in the garage, Joe would surely have seen him go in. He went to the hallway and noticed that the garage had been extended at some time. No doubt to accommodate Micky's love of large cars. The garage jutted about a meter and a half across the hallway window. Joe pulled the curtain back and saw that where the window had been, it had been replaced by a glass door. The glass door opened outwards onto a paved area about six-foot square. Opposite the glass door was a wood door into the garage. It meant that, if he wanted to, he could walk from the house to the garage without anyone seeing him from the street. With an electronic door on the garage, he could be into the car and away in no time.

Joe took his little set of skeleton keys out of his pocket and opened the wood door to the garage. He stepped inside and shone his touch around. There was Micky Naylor, in the centre of the room, hanging from a length of fawn coloured rope. His legs dangled a couple of feet from the ground, and a small step-ladder lay on its side next to him.

An intense feeling of disappointment and anti-climax overcame Joe. His legs felt unsteady, and he had to go and sit down on an old tea chest, which was standing against the wall. This was the moment that he had planned for years. The moment that he would tell Micky just why he was going to die. And now someone had done it for him. He almost felt like crying. He had prepared for himself to become a fugitive, always on the move, never having a home. That was the life he was prepared to live, and now it had been snatched away.

After a while, Joe picked up his things, locked all the doors and went back to the house across the street. He was exhausted. He unrolled his sleeping bag, laid it on top of the very comfortable bed and went to sleep.

CHAPTER 38

Will's anxiety levels had reached a new peak when the telephone rang at home. Emily, Steve and Will had sat down together yesterday to work out a strategy if anyone called him about Lizzie. Emily and Steve were hoping that Lizzie was doing all she could, probably telling them that they would get more money out of Will than they would get from Micky.

They all knew that it was probably not true, but if Will was going to get her back, lies had to be told. The only telephone number that Will could give was his home number. His home was a small, but very nice little flint stone cottage, just a couple of streets behind the Hotel where Emily and Steve were staying.

Will realised that this was the phone number that he had given Lizzie, and she would certainly give it to whoever had taken her and would encourage them to call. She would do that even if it was just to get the message across that she was still alive. There was one slight embarrassment for Will, in that Lizzie had often suggested that they could go there to make love.

Will had always made an excuse about having nosey neighbours, or it not being as nice as her cottage at Salthouse. Both those reasons were sound excuses, but not the whole truth. Will was slightly embarrassed that a twenty-five-year-old man-of-the-world like him still lived at home with his mother.

It did sound bad, but it wasn't really like that at all. Will loved his mother, and she loved him, but she was also his friend. He liked her company and sense of humour and the fact that she never asked where he was going or what he was doing. Ever since his father had died suddenly, from a heart attack five years ago, she had taken over the running of their small crab business, with two boats and a few good regular customers. She augmented that with a little stall she used to erect in the front garden for passing holidaymaker trade. She left all the fishing side of the business for Will to run. And as she had told him many times, he ran it very well.

Will often thought that she must know about his exploits with the young lady holidaymakers, but she never once mentioned it. The problem was that since he met Lizzie, that lifestyle had become history, even though the guys on the boats liked to keep the legend alive. In fact, they had always loved enhancing stories of his exploits, but now he was telling them nothing there was nothing for them to exaggerate.

He had never told his mother about Lizzie because he was afraid that to do so might jinx their relationship. He thought that it was so perfect, it would only work in secret. As luck would have it, his mother had decided to go to the pictures that afternoon, so Will didn't have to challenge the jinx.

But the most important thing now was to get Lizzie, and these other concerns had to be put aside. Emily and Steve were sure that Micky was behind the kidnapping and that he wanted her returned to him. None of those who were sitting there discussing how to get her back wanted to speculate any further than that.

Eric had suggested that he went around all the pubs in the area and asked if anyone knew who they were. He rang Steve, who was still sitting in the bedroom with Emily waiting for someone to call. They were hoping for it to be Will, but hearing from Eric was next best.

He said he had found out something about the men who fitted the description of the two men who followed Emily. Eric said there were usually three of them and they had come to Cromer to help build a barn at a farm near North Walsham. The barn job had fallen through for some reason, and since they had rented a caravan to live in for the four weeks that the job should have taken, they were looking around for any work they could get, to pay for the caravan rent and make a bob or two for themselves.

They kept hanging about, going to several pubs, and asking around. Nobody had seen them for a couple of days, but they were last seen talking to a bloke who matched the description of Micky Naylor.

Emily and Steve were elated that they had at least got confirmation that Micky was behind all this, but as the excitement wore off, they realised that it hadn't got them very far.

They ate some lunch and worried a little more, and then, after two more hours had passed, Will rang them with the news that they were waiting for. A man had called to ask him how much he would pay to get Lizzie back. Will asked him how much he wanted and he said £2,000. Will had said OK and asked him where they should meet and when. Will said that this seemed to throw the caller a bit. He obviously hadn't thought that I would agree so readily. He said that he would have to ring back about the arrangements.

'I hope that was okay,' Will added.

'Yes, absolutely what we wanted Will,' said Steve. 'He needed to think that money wasn't a problem. The work will start for us when we hear where the meet will be. We need as much time as possible to get a strategy worked out, and we can't do that until we know where and when.

It was agreed that Will would stand by the telephone, and Emily and Steve would get as much of the story written as possible because it was going to be a tight deadline. They didn't want to go to press without Lizzie's release. They had to force a conclusion as quickly as possible.

They moved furniture around and turned their bedroom into an office. Their typewriters positioned either side of the large desk, the telephone between them and a large pot of coffee and they were ready to go. It was then that the telephone rang and Emily heard a strange voice from the other end of the line.

'There's someone to see you,' it said in an excitable whisper.

'Who's that?' Asked Emily. She couldn't even tell if it was a male or female voice, it sounded so strange.

'It's Cindy in reception,' she said. 'There's that man in reception asking to talk to you. You know, Nosey Joe. The mystery man,' she added.

'Oh,' said Emily, lost for words for the moment. 'Steve will come down and see him.'

'Steve will come down to see who?' he said, and she put the phone down.

'Joe, the mystery man. He's in reception and I thought you would like to be first to greet him.'

Steve jumped up and made for the door. 'Damn right I would like to meet him. He's been scaring people around the town for long enough; it's time we found out who he is.'

Steve arrived at the reception desk, and Cindy directed him with her eyes, without saying a word. The man was standing just a few yards from the desk, but he was looking out of the hotel front windows. Steve moved around in front of him and said 'Hello, I'm Steve.'

The man appeared to be distracted by something outside, but turned to Steve and said. 'Good of you to see me, Steve, I'm Joe, Joe Jefferies.'

Steve could easily see why Joe had unsettled so many people in the town. He had piercing blue eyes, which seem to lock onto your eyes and almost challenge you to look away.

'How can I help,' said Steve, keeping a friendly tone in his voice.

'You are a journalist, I believe?' Joe said. 'I have a story to tell you about Micky Naylor that I think will interest you. I understand that you are interested in Naylor?' There seemed to be a certain sadness about the man. Steve was not expecting that.

He was expecting the direct, demanding approach that he seemed to have been using on the unsuspecting locals. Steve could well imagine that Joe could be that way. He was just under six feet tall, slightly taller than Steve, but he stood like a man who was confident and ready for action. His hands hung loosely by his side, and he was extremely still and calm.

'Yes,' said Steve, 'we are working on a story about him, but we are also very close to our deadlines, so we don't have much time to spare.'

'What I have to tell you won't take long,' he said. 'I'll keep to the point.'

'Okay, we are using our room here as an office. Come up with me, my partner Emily is up there writing the story now.'

They went up to the room, and he introduced Joe to Emily.

'Joe has a story to tell us, that he thinks will be of interest to us as part of our investigation into Micky Naylor.'

'How did you come to know Micky?' asked Emily, standing up and offering her chair to Joe, while she sat on the end of the bed.

'I have known about him for nearly twenty years, but I never met him until last night.'

'We have never met him,' Steve said.

'Well, saying I met him is not strictly true. I came to Cromer with the intention of meeting him, and I went to his house last night with the intention of killing him, but by the time I got there, he was already dead. Someone beat me to it. And I cannot tell you how disappointed I am.'

Suddenly, Joe had Emily and Steve's full attention.

'Who did kill him,' said Steve.

Joe shrugged his shoulders. 'I don't know. Two guys turned up a couple of hours before I was going to make my move. I don't know who they were or why they were there. I thought they were probably working for Micky. When he wants any dirty work doing he knows plenty of people will do the job for him.

'They parked down the road, which would be sensible if you didn't want to draw attention to the fact that you had to visit Micky. They were there for just over an hour and came out the entrance on the other side of the house. They walked down the alleyway near where the car was parked, jumped in a drove off.'

'What sort of car was it?' Steve asked.

'I decided to go and look at the registration number. I walked down the road and memorised it. This morning I called a friend of mine, who is in the business and got the owner's name. It's registered to Shay Brady. Do you know him.'

'Yes,' said Emily. 'He's one of Micky's men. His right-hand man, we think.'

'So, why did you want him dead?'

'It's a long story, but I will cut it short because you have your deadlines.'

'And another emergency that we are trying to resolve,' said Emily. 'A kidnapping that Micky hired some lunatics to carry out.'

'Whose been kidnapped?' Joe asked.

'Micky's wife. She had left him, and he wanted her back. She knew too much, and he had to silence her.'

'I'll tell you my story, and then I may be able to help you with that.'

Joe quietly and efficiently ran through the story of Micky and Barry's Berlin scam, of Micky's treachery and Barry's suicide. He told them about Micky's return to the UK, with money to start a business and of his own family's distress at Barry's stupidity, shame and then suicide.

He explained that because he was a career soldier, he had decided to put avenging his family honour to the back of his mind until he decided to leave the Army. He took that decision a few months ago and since then had been tracking Naylor down and planning his revenge.

'The main thing that has stuck with me since I heard what had happened in Berlin is that being a soldier is not like working together in civi-street. First and foremost, soldiers have to rely on each other. That is the only way it works. Even if you don't particularly like each other, you watch each other's back. Micky broke that code of honour for a stash of money they had stolen. They should both have faced the music and done their time. Barry would have let the family down, but he would have also been alive to redeem himself.'

The telephone interrupted Joe's story. It was Will. They had called him with a time and a place for the exchange. £2000 for Lizzie and 5.30 tomorrow evening. They were getting anxious about getting their money, and Will wanted Lizzie out of this as soon as possible.

'Come to us at the hotel Will; we are in our room, so come up the back stairs. We have some news for you, and we will make a plan of action.'

CHAPTER 39

Will, Joe, Emily and Steve had talked late into the day about how they were going to go about getting Lizzie back safe and well. They had driven past the field twice, but dare not risk any more than that. The derelict barn stood some way into the field. It was a lone building now, but there were signs that other buildings used to surround it at some time in the past. There was no sign of life, so unless they were in the barn now, which seemed unlikely, they must be holding Lizzie somewhere else.

Joe said that they could not leave it to chance and asked them to drop him off a couple of fields away. He would wait until it was beginning to get dark and then move in and find out if they were in the barn or not. He told them to give him until ten-o-clock and then come back for him at the same place as the drop-off.

The three of them went to find a pub that Will knew in a nearby village. The field with the old barn was about three or four miles inland from Cromer on a well-used minor road. It was a shortcut for local traffic, particularly in summer when it was best to avoid the busy streets of the town.

They sat, largely in silence, and the tension of tomorrow's meeting in that field overshadowed their thoughts. It was too important to waste their time on small talk. They were relieved to have the help of Joe but were also concerned that they had put all their faith into a man they hardly knew. Admittedly, without being in any way boastful, Joe exuded an air of quiet confidence. He looked like a man who expected things to go to plan. That must have been why he was so upset that he had not been able to sit face to face with Micky and tell him why he had to die. That sort of dedication to revenge was way outside the understanding of Will, Emily and Steve, but who knows how you would react to a person who had done a terrible thing to someone you love.

It had become such an obsession for Joe that he was only now able to grasp the fact that his failure was a good thing. Instead of having to become a mercenary, scratching a living fighting other people's wars, he could now make choices in his life.

Will was particularly stressed because it was his beautiful Lizzie who was in the greatest danger. Also, he was the only one who had spoken to Ron, who seems to be so desperate for money, that he was likely to do anything.

It was true what Steve and Joe both said, that Ron and his cronies were amateurs and chancers, but in Will's mind that could be even more dangerous, because you couldn't predict what they were going to do next.

Steve, was calm, but also excited that this was coming to a head. He was confident that Joe knew what he was doing and if they went along with what he said, all would be okay.

Emily was also worried about Lizzie. She could imagine just how Lizzie must be feeling. How awful it must be to be held against your will by three men who were offering to let you live if you paid them enough money. Yes, Lizzie had made many bad choices in life that had led her into this situation. But she had paid for that through a life of hell with Micky. She deserved a break and Emily was sure that Will was the right man for her.

They picked Joe up and headed back to town.

'There's a caravan inside the barn. It's a good idea. I've changed my mind about these guys. They are inexperienced, but not stupid,' Joe said, as soon as he got into the car.

'So, do we need to revise the plan?' asked Steve.

'No, it won't be a problem,' Joe said but didn't elaborate.

'And what about the money, that I don't have?' asked Will.

'No problem,' said Joe. 'Just a small holdall with something in it or a shopping bag. It doesn't matter. They are not going to get to look at it.'

CHAPTER 40

They arrived five minutes early and parked in front of the five-bar gate that led into the field where the barn stood. Now they were getting a proper look at it; the fact that it was still standing at all was quite remarkable.

Emily, who was driving the hire car that Steve had rented, looked for signs of life around the barn. She noticed that the whole structure was leaning to the left and the double doors that she could just see at one end of the barn, had detached themselves from the main structure. There was a gap at the top of the door frame, where the barn leant away from the door, but at the bottom, the doors and the barn were still holding together.

Emily's job was to sit in the car, and if she saw anything happening around the field that Joe, Will and Steve couldn't see, she was to sound the car horn in one long blast.

There were still four minutes to go until 5.30, but she noticed the door open a little and a head poke out and look towards the car.

'They must be as keen as we are to get on with this, so let's not keep them waiting,' Joe said as if they were off to have a nice chat with someone. Joe, Will and Steve got out the car and climbed over the gate, Joe carrying the holdall.

Immediately, Emily saw the tall, thin one called Ron begin to run towards Joe, Will and Steve.

'I said you had to come alone,' he screamed.

'Now that wouldn't be fair, would it,' Joe said in a big booming voice. 'Three of us and three of you. That's how it's going to be if you don't want me to come over there and rip your bollocks off. Come on, do you want the money or not? £2000 is a lot of money.' He waved the bag in his hand.

Ron stopped in his tracks, looked bemused. He didn't expect aggression when as he saw it, he was carrying the trump card – Lizzie.

'Come on,' Joe shouted again. 'Here's the money let's see the girl. If you've harmed her in any way, this will be a day you will never forget until the end of your miserable lives.'

Joe, Will and Steve had been walking steadily towards Ron, and now they quickened their pace to put the pressure on Ron to react. The barn doors opened a little more, and two men came out carrying what looked like a body between them. Emily gave a small scream and said quietly to herself, 'Oh no, they haven't killed her.'

But almost immediately. The body came to life and began to kick and twist against the men who were holding her. The stocky one made a grab to hold her still, but it seemed just to set a madness off in her. She pulled her legs away from the other man and turned onto Bert. She was screaming and shouting and clawed at his face until the other man pulled her off him.

Lizzie looked in a dreadful state, but she obviously hadn't lost her spirit. She was dressed in a now rather torn man's shirt and was barefooted. The two men settled for Lizzie walking between them, while they held onto each arm.

The little group met and stopped.

'Okay, that's close enough, said Ron.

Joe said nothing.

'Let me see the money,' Ron said.

Joe still said nothing. He just walked up to Ron and dropped it on the floor. Ron bent down to open it, and in one movement Joe kicked Ron in the face, not hard, but enough to make him yell and stand up. Joe then stepped forward and hit him low down on the body, but with full force. Ron went down like he had been pole-axed and lay writhing on the floor.

Bert and Alf stood looking stunned.

'Let her go,' said Joe, very quietly.

Alf did as he was told immediately, but Bert made a grab at Lizzie. She pulled away just as Joe arrived and landed a solid punch to Bert's face. He went down on his knees blood coming from his nose and mouth, plus a couple of teeth.

Lizzie ran to Will, and they clung to each other, both crying, both happy.

Ron was making an effort to stand up, but his body wasn't ready for that yet.

Bert was making whimpering and snuffling noises as he remained on his knees.

They turned and walked away as Alf went over to the bag and opened it, Joe turned and watched him picking out the old newspapers that they had stuffed in the bag. He kept pulling the papers out as if he still hoped to find £2000 hidden underneath.

'There's nothing here,' Alf shouted. 'Where is the money?'

Joe turned and looked at Alf. 'Just be pleased that we haven't called the police, yet. You have still got your freedom, which is more than you deserve. Go home and be thankful that we are such forgiving people.' shouted Joe as they walked away.

CHAPTER 41

Shay Brady called Sergeant Brian Brooks from London to say that he was concerned about Micky Naylor's state of mind and that he had tried, without success to contact him, so could the police please go round and check on him.

It was, of course, a pre-arranged call that Brooks could then log the call and Shay's alibi was properly established. Brooks also knew that their journey to Naylor's house would discover Naylor hanging in his garage, because of worries about his business and his marriage break-up.

After Shay put the phone down, he wondered what Sergeant Brooks would do next. He didn't know that they were going to move operations elsewhere. Brooks was one of Naylor's men and even though he had played it straight with them this time, Guus never really trusted anyone except those he chose himself.

He couldn't take his story to anyone because to do so he would only destroy himself. Shay would go back to Norfolk tomorrow and then talk to Nick and Guus and decide where to go. Shay wanted somewhere that you could be anonymous and the people weren't so damn friendly.

When Shay got back to Cromer, he tried to contact Nick, but the phone appeared to have been disconnected. He needed to contact Nick urgently to discuss where they were going to move their operations to. He drove to Wells, but when he knocked on the door, no one came.

He looked through the front window, and there was no sign of life inside.'

'They have gone away,' a voice came from the next-door garden, but Shay could not see anyone.

Then he saw a grey-haired head rise above the rose bush. A tiny old lady, with watering can in hand stood up, but she was only just higher than the rose bush.

'They went, yesterday,' she said in a very quiet voice. 'It was very sudden. Kiki came and said goodbye and they were gone. I'm going to miss her. She was a lovely young woman.'

'Oh, well, sorry to hear that. I only dropped in on the off-chance, as I was passing by.'

Shay got quickly back into his car and drove away. Now it had happened, he was not really surprised. Nick was never really cut out for this sort of business. And he was very protective of Kiki.

Nick would have found it difficult to tell Kiki what had happened to Micky. He wondered if Guus knew about this in advance. No, Nick wouldn't take the risk. He would have had this planned for years. And an escape plan that Nick created would be perfect. Shay would guess that it involved Malaya, but who knows?

Lizzie had hardly slept for three nights. She had been stuck in that smelly old caravan, wearing a man's shirt and no shoes. She had been groped by Bert, who broke out in a sweat every time he saw her. She had been scared out of her mind that she would be sold back to Micky and worried about what had happened to Will.

It was not surprising that she just couldn't stop crying on the way home in the car. They were not 'feeling sorry for herself tears' or 'look what those nasty men did to me' tears. They were tears of happiness that she was suddenly free and was with Will. She couldn't feel in any way sad that Micky was dead. It was what he deserved after all the lives he had destroyed. She didn't for a moment believe the suicide story, but if that's what people wanted to say it was okay with her.

When they got back to the hotel, Steve got rooms for Will and Lizzie and Joe. They all deserved a couple of days to recover, and he and Emily wanted them close by so they could finish their stories and get them to Martin. Steve would, of course, charge the extra rooms to expenses, but they were getting an exclusive story that was certainly going to boost their circulation.

Two days later and everything was complete. Steve and Emily had finished the stories and sent them to Martin. When they had arrived in Cromer, they were both sceptical that there was a story to be told. And even if there was, the chances of getting to the truth did not look promising. The breakthrough came when Lizzie walked out on Micky. It was a brave thing to do, and it could have gone badly wrong. Lizzie and Will were now planning their new life together in Cromer. They were talking about expanding the crab business and selling direct to hotels and restaurants. Lizzie even allowed herself to think about a reconciliation with her family. Once the inevitable sensationalism of the story died down, she was sure that her father would welcome her and Will back into the family.

Joe was also planning to turn his life around. He realised that revenge came at a price and that he was very lucky that he was too late to vent his years of anger on Micky. The years of suppressed hate had turned him into a weird recluse, with no friends and no ambition. Now he had four friends with Emily, Steve, Lizzie and Will and they all promised to keep in touch. Steve had suggested that they tell his story as a background piece to the main story about Micky Naylor. They could make Joe's intentions clear, but gloss over the fact that he was sitting in the house opposite, ready to kill Micky. Steve said it would look good on his CV when he went for another job.

Having said their goodbyes Steve and Emily went to visit Steve's mother at the B&B. They had kept their distance from her throughout the investigation because the last thing they wanted was for her to get dragged into what they were doing.

Iris said she had been hearing from her next-door neighbour some of the things that had been happening and she had been worried about them. Steve and Emily laughed it off as being just a routine job for them and that was how it felt.

But always at the back of their minds were the what-ifs. What if they hadn't managed to get Lizzie back? What if Joe hadn't taken control of the exchange, could they have handled that? What if Will hadn't managed to convince Lizzie to meet them and tell them all she knew?

They stayed and had lunch with Iris and arranged to come and stop for a few days over Christmas. They said their goodbyes and drove home.

The end.

18220112R00164

Printed in Great Britain
by Amazon